Varun's Quest

Into a Bee Tree and Other Adventures

Timothy H. Goldsmith

ILLUSTRATIONS BY Julia S. Child

For Lizzy, who saw the plate before Aubrey was ready to receive visitors, and Varun, who did the exploring for both of them.

Author's Foreword

ON MY EIGHTH CHRISTMAS I was given a copy of Children of the Sea by Wilfrid S. Bronson, a charming story of the intertwined lives of a dolphin and a small boy from Nassau on New Providence Island. The interaction between boy and dolphin was exciting and almost believable, but I was enchanted by the author's descriptions of the variety of animals and the aquatic environments through which the story moved. The backwaters of the Florida everglades, the Gulf Stream, the tide pools and coral reefs of South Florida and the Bahamas all provided distinct habitats whose creatures were interestingly described and profusely illustrated by the author's careful drawings.

The memory of this book, indeed the book itself, has remained with me to this day and has led me to believe that fantasy, carefully used, can bring the excitement of scientific discovery to young children. I owe many thanks to a group of Connecticut authors, both published and struggling, who write for children, meet regularly in Guilford and Madison, listen to passages of each other's work, and offer constructive suggestions. Their cheerful input helped me navigate more than one tricky shoal. Although the ultimate judgment rests with children, I believe that Varun's Quest has much to share with parents and grandparents. And I am gratified by the judgments of several scientists, science writers and science educators, each of whom has contributed to the ongoing task of transforming science education and the cultivation of scientific literacy.

Praise for *Varun's Quest*

"*Varun's Quest* is a wonderful book, a combination of fantasy and science, with real episodes by a real scientist—altogether a 21st century book for the young."
—Edward O. Wilson, University Research Professor Emeritus, Harvard University.

"Said one young reader of this book, 'It's a pretend story about real stuff.' Goldsmith weaves a young boy's adventures with an Elf with clear but age-appropriate science to present an engaging tale about 'real stuff' that will both educate and stimulate."
—Eugenie Scott, Executive Director, National Center for Science Education.

"A lovely story that introduces children to nature, and to all that can be learned about it with an inquiring mind."
—Carl Zimmer, popular science writer, blogger of The Loom, and author of *Evolution: The Triumph of an Idea* and other books.

"This remarkable account of a child's exploration of science and nature should be read by anyone thinking about reforming education."
—Donald Kennedy, President Emeritus and Bing Professor of Environmental Sciences Emeritus, Stanford University.

"As parents and teachers search for ways to implement the Common Core State Standards for the English language arts, they will discover that *Varun's Quest* is a wonderful example of a fictional story that provides a science narrative in a well-written, brightly illustrated, and meaningful context for children."
—Rodger Bybee, Science Educator and Consultant, Executive Director Emeritus, Biological Sciences Curriculum Study.

"*Varun's Quest* is a wonderful story that kept me engaged from beginning to end. There is real magic in nature to be enjoyed by both children and adults. What a shame that our standard textbooks instead make learning a chore. In Varun's Quest, not only does the magic stand out, but the science sticks with you effortlessly. And the drawings are perfect."
—Bruce Alberts, Editor-in-Chief of *Science* magazine, President Emeritus, The National Academy of Sciences, Professor Emeritus of Biochemistry and Biophysics, University of California San Francisco.

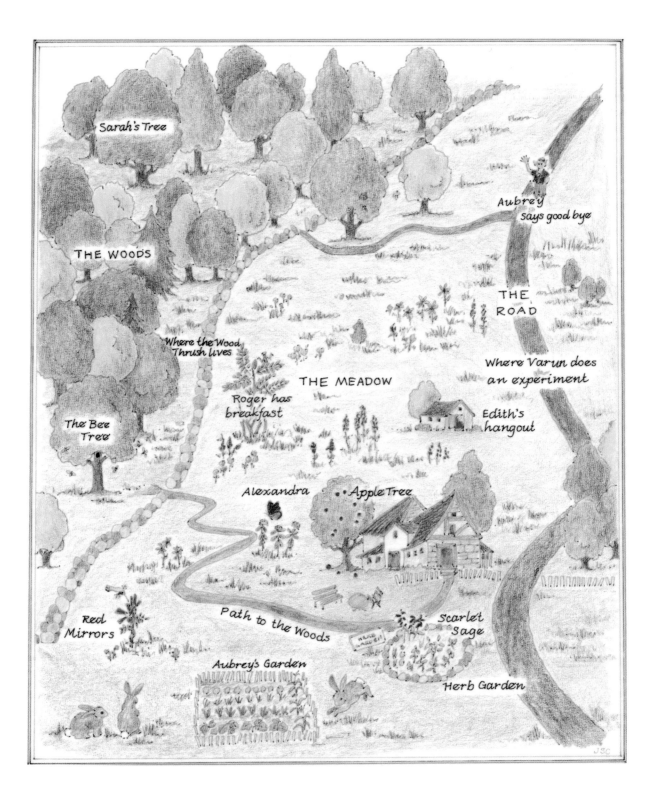

Contents

Varun's Quest

CHAPTER 1

Wherein We Meet Varun and a Mysterious Dinner Plate

Grandpa could be something of a tease, but on one occasion events took a turn that Varun could not have imagined. It all began on a warm summer evening. The western sky was washed with orange from the setting sun, and the water in the harbor glowed in the reflection. Varun was curled up on the sofa with an electronic game in his hand, intent on getting his race car across the finish line in record time, when Grandpa pointed to the garden.

"Varun, it's always busy out here at this time of day. There are monarch butterflies on the flowers and a hummingbird at the feeder. A big spider has just built a web in the blueberry bush, too. They're all looking for a snack before it gets dark. When it gets a bit darker the bats will also be hunting. And look, there's even a swarm of bees in the apple tree."

"Oh, Grandpa! Not right now." Varun's race car survived a sharp curve, accelerated down a straightaway, and he continued jabbing at the controls.

Grandpa smiled and went to the dish cupboard. He took out one of the plates, brought it to the sofa, and sat next to Varun. Varun sighed as his race car careened into a ditch. He rolled his eyes, put down his game, and gave Grandpa a slice of his attention.

"Look at this plate." Grandpa pointed. "You and I are in this picture."

Varun had seen the plate before — white, with a country scene in green, and a cottage by the side of a dirt road. He thought the place seemed far away, perhaps in an earlier time, and he had sometimes wondered if it were a real place and who lived there. Now, as Grandpa called his attention to two tiny figures on the road, Varun studied them carefully. One was larger than the other, and closer, and had a hat with a big brim, but he couldn't tell much about them, even which way they were walking. Still frustrated by the fate of his race car, he was not quite ready for one of Grandpa's goofy jokes.

"Oh sure, that's you and me," he muttered.

"You and I," said Grandpa.

Everyone in the family tried to ignore Grandpa when he fussed about words, and Varun found it easy now. Those plates had been in the cupboard as long as he could remember, and as far as he knew they were there before he was born.

"That's silly, Grandpa. That plate is too old for me to be in the picture."

"Don't be so sure about what you think you see on this plate. That's a special place, and I'd like to take you there some time." Grandpa sounded very serious.

"Where is it, then?"

"It's much closer than it seems. It's also a place best appreciated by the curious."

Just then Grandma brought in some ice cream, and everyone's attention turned to fudge sauce and sprinkles.

Later, as Varun crawled into bed for the night, he began to think about what Grandpa had said. Being in a picture on that plate was nonsense, but was that a real place? And what did Grandpa mean when he said it was a place best appreciated by the curious? Grandpa made silly jokes, but sometimes he could be very serious, and sometimes you weren't quite sure what he was up to. Varun yawned and came to a decision. Tomorrow I'll ask him what he meant by that being a place for the curious.

He turned and gazed out the window. A full moon brightened the night. Big, billowy, low-lying clouds raced across the moon on a brisk breeze that was shaking the leaves on the horse chestnut tree in the yard. Varun's dreamy thoughts drifted to where the wind might be coming from and where it might be going. The clouds seemed to him like of a train of enormous pillows speeding along invisible tracks, and he wondered what it would be like if clouds could carry passengers and where the clouds might take them. He smiled to himself as he imagined settling into a cloud-pillow as the engineer. His eyes closed in sleep….

He felt as if he were moving…and when he looked over the edge of a cloud, the land was racing by underneath him….The cloud rolled gently… and Varun felt himself falling…ever so slowly….

CHAPTER 2

A New Friend and
Two Pairs of Amazing Ears

S uddenly Varun was standing at the side of a dusty road. Surprised, he quickly looked around to see where he was. The road wound through countryside with fields and woodlands as far as the eye could see. He had no idea where he was, but even though he seemed to be by himself, he didn't feel the least bit frightened. Was he dreaming? A hard pinch convinced him he was wide awake, and he began to look around more carefully. He was sure he had never been here before, but nevertheless the place felt familiar, particularly the cottage on the other side of the road. The picture on the plate flashed through his mind. That's ridiculous, he decided. People don't climb in and out of dinner plates!

A movement drew his attention to a small figure sitting on the door step, knees pulled up under his chin and arms folded around his legs. But the clothes were the strangest Varun had ever seen. An apple-green shirt was partly covered by a bright purple jacket with bold brass buttons. Blue knickers gave way below the knees to a pair of long, pale orange stockings and blue shoes with buckles, the whole topped off with a little blue cap sporting a red feather. Varun took him for a boy who lived in the cottage, and he waved a hesitant hand.

"Hello, Varun. I've been expecting you," came the response.

The voice was friendly, but not the voice of a child, and for a fleeting moment, Varun thought it sounded familiar. He crossed the road and walked tentatively through the gate of a little picket fence. As he came closer, he saw that although the figure was almost his size and the face looked young, the hair was gray. The broad smile, however, was reassuring, and Varun approached closer. Most unusual of all were the ears. They were not only large, they were pointed, and twitched and swiveled about.

"What are you?" blurted Varun.

"I'm an Elf," said the voice in an important-sounding way. "You can call me Aubrey."

Varun was not about to fall for that line. "Elves are make-believe!"

"I'm real enough."

"Real enough? What do you mean by that?"

"Look here," said the Elf. "Lots of people believe in things that aren't really real. And when they really believe in them, those things are very real to the believer. Understand?"

This was confusing, but so was the whole idea of meeting an Elf. "I'm not sure," Varun replied, being at a loss for anything smarter to say.

"Well, no matter, it's philosophy. The important thing is you're here, and it's time to have fun."

Varun was up for fun, particularly as it seemed much more agreeable than philosophy. But as the Elf had not moved, he was not sure what to say next. "I thought Aubrey was a girl's name," was the best he could manage.

"It's an old and honorable elfin name for boys," said the Elf, straightening up and looking prim. "You can look that up when you get home."

That had not gone well either, so Varun decided on another approach. "Do you live in this house?"

"Not all the time. This is where I entertain guests like you."

Varun was not sure he was being entertained, so he tried once more. "Why are your ears so big?" As soon as the words were out of his mouth, he realized that his question sounded rude. He hoped the Elf would not be offended.

The Elf apparently thought the matter of ears was self-evident. "To hear better. What did you suppose?"

Varun considered this briefly. "I can hear perfectly well, and my ears aren't nearly as big."

"Ah, ha," retorted the Elf. "Do you think you can hear everything there is to hear?"

This was something Varun had never thought about. "I don't know," he said.

"You can't hear the flight of an owl as it glides through the forest in search of mice. And you can't hear the high-pitched cries of bats. Watch this."

The Elf seemed to be saying something. His mouth moved, but Varun couldn't hear any sound. The Elf pointed to the top of the house, and a bat flew out from under the edge of the roof.

"What do you want?" it demanded in a grumpy squeal. "You know I sleep during the day." The bat's voice was so high Varun could hardly make it out.

"I'm sorry, William, but we have company today. Varun, this is William."

The bat fluttered in front of Varun for a moment, sighed as though resigned to the Elf's whims, and spoke. "Hello, Varun."

Varun blinked in disbelief.

The bat had very big ears, so big they seemed much too large for the rest of its head, but its eyes were tiny. And when it opened its mouth Varun saw some very sharp teeth.

Varun had never been addressed by a bat before, but now that it had happened, he thought courtesy required some sort of response. All he could manage was "Do you really fly around at night?" His voice was shrill, and he was startled by the sound. Furthermore, the question sounded dumb. "How do you keep from bumping into things?" he added.

"Oh, for goodness sake, Aubrey", complained the bat. "Is this a show-and-tell? You know I was up all night. Why don't you tell him? I want to go back to bed."

"Don't be so impatient, William. We won't keep you long." The Elf handed Varun a small pebble. "Hold it so William can see what I gave you."

Varun held out his hand with the little stone in his palm.

"William, can you see what Varun has in his hand?"

"See? You know very well I'm legally blind. And I can barely see anything in this bright light."

"Okay, Varun, throw that thing I gave you up in the air as high as you can so William can catch it."

Varun cocked his arm and tossed the pebble as high as he could. The bat was after it in a flash and was on it before it started to fall to the ground. At the last moment, William turned aside.

"Ugh!" he shrilled. "That wasn't anything to eat! It's as hard as a rock! I bet it was a little rock. I really am going back to bed." And with that he disappeared into the hole under the roof.

Varun was astonished by what had just happened. "I didn't know animals could talk," he said.

"They can't talk as you and I do."

"But I heard you speak to that bat, and he answered you! And I'm sure he was talking to me."

The Elf smiled, but his words left Varun more mystified than ever. "If you study animals carefully, you begin to understand them in new and wonderful ways. And if you are very clever, they may let you in on their secrets. Perhaps that is what you heard."

CHAPTER 3

Bouncing Balls and
Bouncing Voices

Meeting an Elf was mystery enough, but a bat that talked to him? Or had it really? And the Elf seemed to be speaking in riddles. Nevertheless, Varun was curious about the bat, even if he didn't understand everything Aubrey said.

"If William really is almost blind, how did he chase that pebble? He could have caught it if he had wanted."

Instead of answering, the Elf reached into a big canvas bag sitting next to the doorstep. He took out a rubber ball and began to bounce it on the ground.

"Do you know what an echo is?"

Varun was relieved to be asked something he knew. "Of course! Sometimes if you are standing in a big space and yell HELLO, your voice will come back to you from a wall or cliff. You hear your own voice say 'hello' a second after you yell."

"That's good. An echo is a bounce of sound, just like the bounce of a ball. William was making sounds all the time he was flying around. They were loud, but you couldn't hear them because they were so high. William could not only hear them, he could hear their echoes."

"You mean that's how he chased the pebble I threw into the air? And how he knew it wasn't something to eat when he got close to it?" Varun was suspicious the Elf was kidding him.

"Exactly so."

"But why does he use such a high voice that I can't hear it?"

"The fact that you can't hear it is of no matter to William. Your ears aren't built for listening to your own echoes, and his are." The Elf looked thoughtful and scratched an ear. "To be sure, some people like to hear the sound of their own voice with or without an echo."

Yeah, thought Varun. Just like you!

"But it sounds better if they know what they are talking about," the Elf concluded with a wink. "Now, let's play a game."

Aubrey pulled the bag over to a clear spot about ten steps away from the picket fence and got out several more balls. "Let's see who can bounce a ball off that fence."

Varun saw the challenge. The balls were small enough that if they didn't hit one of the wooden pickets, they would go through the spaces between the pickets. He looked at the Elf carefully. He was taller than Aubrey, and if they were going to have a contest, it would be best if he could beat him. He smiled to himself as he picked up five balls. When he threw them, however, only two bounced back. The other three went through the spaces between the boards.

Varun was feeling a bit uncertain about the outcome of the 'contest' when it dawned on him that maybe the Elf was up to something. "Does this have anything to do with William's echoes?"

"It sure does," said Aubrey. "Suppose William wants to know whether there is anything where that fence is. He can't see the fence at night, but he can aim his voice at it, like this." He threw two balls, and they both bounced off the same picket. Then he walked back about ten feet and hit the same picket with the third ball.

"That's good aim," said Varun. "Mine isn't that good." The Elf was beginning to impress him, and he was glad that the 'contest' was only in his own head. At least Aubrey wouldn't be boasting about winning or making fun of him.

"So sounds bounce like balls," said Varun. "And an echo tells William there is something solid there?"

The Elf nodded. "It's called echolocation."

In a flash, Varun had another idea. "The closer you were to the fence, the quicker the ball came back to you. I bet it's the same for an echo, and that's how the bat knows how far away something is."

"Good thinking," agreed the Elf. "Now suppose William wants to know whether that object is wide like a wall or narrow like the trunk of a little tree. He aims his voice a bit to the left, and then a bit to the right. Like this."

Aubrey threw two more balls, one into the space on each side of the picket. "See? No bounce, no echo."

"But I still don't understand why the bat uses such a high voice" said Varun.

Aubrey reached into the bag and took out a ball that was much larger than the width of a single picket. "What do you think would happen if we threw this at the fence?" he asked.

"It doesn't fit into the spaces between the boards, so it will bounce back".

"Good. Throwing small balls and catching their bounces is like speaking in a high voice and hearing the echoes. But throwing a large ball is like speaking in a low voice." He threw the large ball, and they watched it bounce back.

"I get it," said Varun. "William's voice has to be so high for him to tell little things from big things by listening to his own echoes."

"Congratulations, Varun. That's a sound conclusion," Aubrey laughed. "Get it? It's a sound conclusion."

Varun winced. He was thinking Yeah, and you sound just like Grandpa.

The Elf continued chuckling. "Sound conclusion. Oh that's good!" He finally pulled himself together and came back to the bat. "Sounds are waves in the air, waves of air pressure. You can't see them like you see ripples in a pond. Low sounds have long waves; high sounds have short waves. Short waves bounce off of small things like small balls do. Your voice is much

lower than the sounds William uses to locate things by their echoes. If he had your voice, the smallest thing he could locate would be bigger than you."

"I get it. His voice is so high he can catch little insects in the air," said Varun. "That's pretty cool."

"Right. Throwing balls is cool. Discovering new and interesting things is cool, too. There are many different kinds of cool. That's more philosophy."

Discovering how bats get around without bumping into things had certainly been fun, but at the mention of philosophy, Varun wanted to change the subject. "What shall we do next?" he asked.

The Elf smiled. "Would you like to meet another of my friends?"

CHAPTER 4

A Most Unusual Experience

Varun was fascinated by discovering how bats make their way around at night by listening to the echoes of their own cries, and now he was eager to meet more of the Elf's friends. Aubrey led the way to a garden behind the cottage, and Varun was surprised to see so many different kinds of flowers, many in full bloom. They ranged from asters to zinnias, each labeled by name. Varun could see every color in the rainbow, along with purple and white. The garden was also alive with insects, mostly bees and butterflies, all visiting the flowers.

"This is nice," said Varun, "but what game are we going to play now?"

"It's a form of seek and you will find."

"What do you mean?"

"You can't expect to find before you seek," said the Elf, as though that explained everything.

"I wish you weren't so hard to understand."

The Elf's response only deepened the mystery. "Elves are often that way. You were sent to me for a purpose, and ours is a game of discovery."

"What are we supposed to discover?"

"If you knew that ahead of time, there would be no discovery to make, would there? Think of it as a quest."

"How do you play? What are the rules?"

"I'm the organizer and referee. I'll present you with opportunities and challenges. Sometimes I will provide you with clues to guide your quest. And sometimes I will even make new rules as we go along."

This was the strangest game Varun had ever heard, and he was not sure he liked the idea of changing the rules in the middle of the game, especially if he wasn't the one to make the changes. "Am I going to have fun?"

"I think you enjoyed William."

William had both astonished and puzzled Varun, and the bat was a reminder that the Elf was no ordinary companion. Varun decided if Aubrey was going to be so mysterious, it would be easiest to wait to see what would happen next. But he had another question.

"What do you mean, I was sent here?"

"Should you complete your quest successfully, that will become clear at the end." The Elf put his hands on Varun's shoulders and looked into his eyes. "Now, here is rule number one: You can see a lot just by looking."

Varun laughed. Aubrey was much easier to talk to when he was being funny. "I guess that's more philosophy, isn't it?"

"A famous philosopher said that, and it's very good philosophy. It's the first rule for trying to figure out how the world works. If you're a good observer, you can discover many things wherever you happen to be." He left that idea for Varun to ponder as they walked farther into the garden, and Varun wondered what was coming next.

They stopped at a pair of stools next to group of blue flowers, alive with visiting bees. Aubrey sat and invited Varun to join him. "Let's see how good an observer you are," he said. "How many legs does a bee have?"

Varun looked at one of the bees carefully. "I count six. I think all insects have six legs."

"Right. What else do you see when you look at a bee?"

"Well there's a head. And then a middle part where the legs and wings are attached, and then there is a big part on the rear end with yellow and black bands around it." Varun was hoping there would be more to the game than this!

"The middle part is called the thorax. Do you have a thorax?"

"I don't know."

"Well you do. That's a fancy name for your chest. The big part on the back end of the bee is called the abdomen."

Varun laughed. "My abdomen is my tummy, and my food goes there."

"It's pretty much the same for the bee. Now, perhaps you would like to meet one of these bees up close?"

Varun's first thought was that he did not want to be stung, and he hesitated. "You mean closer than this?"

The Elf rose from his stool and motioned for Varun to stand. "I mean eyeball to compound eye. Here, take my hand."

As Varun grasped Aubrey's hand, he was about to ask what a compound eye was, but the words never left his mouth. Suddenly the world exploded in size. When he had recovered his senses, he was still standing next to Aubrey, but they were both dwarfed by the plants in the garden, which now seemed enormous. As Varun looked around, however, he decided the sizes of the plants, the two stools, and everything else he could see were in proper proportion to each other. He concluded he and the Elf were now very small, and the realization frightened him.

"If you climb up this stem, you'll get a really close look," said Aubrey.

This was a challenge, and Varun's fear began to fade. He started to climb the closest stem.

The Elf set a nimble pace up a neighboring stem. "Mind your manners and you won't get into trouble," he called in a cheerful voice.

Varun climbed more slowly, finding sturdy resting places where leaves were attached, and using hair-like projections on the stem as hand- and footholds in the places between leaves. When he had climbed a couple of feet and reached the flowers, he saw the Elf sitting on a leaf of a nearby plant.

"I'll wait here and watch. If you stay next to that flower, you'll be able to meet a bee up close," Aubrey instructed.

CHAPTER 5

Varun Meets a Bee

Now reduced to the size of an insect and having climbed the stem of a flower, Varun crawled onto the blossom in order to smell it. Suddenly a loud buzzing arrived next to his head. Startled, he jumped back and almost fell off the petals. An enormous honey bee flew in front of him, settled on the flower, and turning, glared at him.

"My flower," it demanded in a buzzy voice.

It took Varun a moment to remember the bee was not extraordinarily large. But as he was much smaller than normal, he did not want to have any trouble. "I only smelled it," he said. He was surprised at the sound of his voice. His words had the same buzzy sound the bee had made when it spoke to him.

"Hmmm", said the bee. "Stand aside while I sample this one." It unhinged the front of its face and thrust it deep into the flower.

Varun chuckled. Nothing like my tongue, he thought.

The bee put its face back together and stepped back on the petal. "Very good nectar," it murmured to itself. "High sugar content." Then it brushed a crumb of pollen from its face with one of its front legs.

The bee appeared to be in a better mood now, and Varun tried to start a conversation. "Do you always clean your face with your feet?"

Varun seemed to have put his own foot in his mouth, because the bee turned and glared. "What on earth are you talking about?"

Startled, Varun wasn't at all sure what he was talking about and fell back on familiar words. "I mean, we are supposed to wipe our face with a napkin if we have smeared food all over it," he said in a weak voice.

"I have cleaning tools on my front legs. I have a couple of brushes and a little ring to clean my antennae. I'm very well put together. By the way, what's a napkin?"

"Oh never mind. I suppose each kind of creature does things in its own way." Varun was looking intently at the rows of tiny bristles on the bee's leg that she used as brushes. Then, hoping to strike a more positive note he added. "My name is Varun. What's yours?"

"I'm Elizabeth, but you can call me Lizzy. It sounds buzzier" The bee was also sounding friendlier.

"Would you mind if I tried some of your nectar?"

"Go ahead," said the bee. "There's not much left."

Varun stuck his hand deep within the flower and moistened his fingers. He pulled out his hand, licked sweetness from his fingers, and wiped off the rest on his shirt.

"Ha!" said the bee. "You criticized me for cleaning my face with my prothoracic tarsus. And what do you do? First you stick your front leg in your mouth and lick it, then you wipe off what's left on that floppy skin you have. I guess different creatures do have different manners."

"That's not my front leg, it's my arm, and this isn't my skin, it's a T-shirt."

"Whatever," said the bee. "It's dirty now, and who is going to clean it? If you lived where I do, you wouldn't be allowed to be so untidy."

"You're not so neat yourself," Varun countered. "You're all covered with yellow stuff!"

"Oh that," said the bee. "That happens. It's hard to collect nectar without getting dusted by those sacks of pollen in the anthers. It doesn't matter what kind of flower I visit, the anthers are always in the way. But nobody really cares, because pollen is good to eat."

Varun thought he couldn't get away with a flimsy excuse like that, but he held his tongue as the bee babbled on.

"The young bees really need pollen, and I was just going to put some in my pollen baskets to take home."

With that, she packed loose pollen under stiff hairs on her rear legs until her baskets were so full she had a big yellow lump on each of her two hindmost legs.

"Can I ask you a question?" said Varun. "It's sort of personal," he added as he realized he might upset the bee again.

"I suppose so. You don't seem to know much."

"Are those long, skinny things on your head your antennae? What do you do with them?"

Lizzy laughed. "You really don't know much. I use my antennae to smell flowers and touch things to find out more about them. Can you really smell flowers? I don't see how you can. You don't have antennae"

Varun was tempted to say that Lizzy didn't know everything either, but he thought better of it. "I smell things with my nose." He demonstrated by taking a deep sniff of the flower. "This smells really good."

"Sometimes I don't have to see it in order to tell what shape something is," Lizzy boasted. "I can tell by flying over it and smelling it. I have to admit, though, I can tell better by looking at it."

"What do you mean you can tell the shape of things by smelling?" Varun thought the bee was taking him for a doofus.

"My smell receivers are out in the open, on my antennae. That makes smelling almost like touching. Yours are inside your head, so you can't get really close to the source of an odor. You have to suck air into your nose, and the odors in the air get all mixed together."

That was a new idea for Varun, and he decided to let Lizzy have the last word on sniffing and smelling. "Those big, black, pebbly things on your face, are those eyes? They don't look anything like my eyes."

"I have compound eyes."

"What does that mean?"

"Each of those little rounded facets on the surface of my eye is a tiny

lens. The lenses all look in slightly different directions, and my brain puts the tiny spots of light together to make a single view of the world. I can see colors, too. I find flowers by smelling their fragrance and seeing their colors."

Varun had never realized there were such different ways of seeing and smelling, and he wanted to know more about the bee. "Tell me what it's like where you live," he said. "Do you have any sisters or brothers?"

The bee gave him another pitying look. "I have thousands of sisters."

"Thousands?"

"Thousands. Too many to keep count. And right now I have a couple hundred brothers. We call them drones; big fat idle things they are."

Varun was incredulous. "But how does your mother take care of all those kids?"

"She doesn't do any housework or child care," said the bee in a scornful tone. "She lays eggs. And when the eggs hatch, my younger sisters take care of the larvae until they turn into bees with wings like mine."

"You don't take care of the baby bees? What do you do?"

"Not baby bees, you bumpkin. Larvae. Even though I don't work in the nursery any more, I can show it to you if you come to my house. I collect nectar and pollen from flowers now! But I'm sorry I can't stay here any longer and talk. Bees like to stay busy. If you come to the bee tree, look for me. I'll be glad to see you again." With that she was off on a buzz of wings.

CHAPTER 6

How a Plant Is Like a Chicken

"Well, what did you think of that?" said Aubrey from his perch on a neighboring stem.

"That was great," said Varun, delighted to have met a bee in such intimate circumstances, but also relieved that he had not been stung.

"I'll bet you didn't know flies taste with their feet," said Aubrey. "Suppose you had to put your bare feet on your dinner to find out how it tastes?"

Varun laughed. "That would be gross."

"Indeed," said the Elf. "Now, here's a question for you. Why do you suppose flowers are brightly colored, smell nice, and make nectar?"

"Lizzy said that was how she finds flowers, so she can get nectar and pollen."

"Ahh," said Aubrey. "But why are the plants inviting insects to come to their flowers?"

Varun was puzzled. "You mean what's in it for the plants?"

"Now you're thinking," said the Elf.

"Well, I guess you mean it isn't a free lunch for the bees," said Varun. He thought for a moment. "Lizzy was all covered with pollen, and she said she couldn't help it, and I could see why. The flower was shaped so Lizzy got dusted every time she came for nectar."

"Have you ever heard of pollination?" Aubrey asked.

"I think it has something to do with making seeds and new plants," said Varun. "Oh, I get it. The bee gets all dusty and carries pollen around with it when it goes to other flowers. It's like when I walk in mud and Mom gets mad if I come inside with dirty shoes. Except the flowers don't care 'cause they really want the pollen."

"Do you know what an egg is?" Aubrey asked.

"You get it from a chicken and eat it for breakfast," said Varun, laughing.

"Suppose you didn't eat it?" said Aubrey.

"You could hard-boil it and have it for lunch," said Varun, laughing harder.

"Very funny," said the Elf. "If you left the egg with the hen, what would happen?"

"Well, I guess it would hatch into a chick."

"Right. Do plants have eggs?"

"I don't know. I've never seen one."

"They're tiny and way down inside the flower. They are really called ovules, which just means little egg. Eggs have to be fertilized before they can make a new plant or animal."

"I bet that's what the pollen does." said Varun.

"Right again. Pollen is in those little sacks called anthers. Bees and other insects carry pollen to other flowers. Pollen that lands on the stigma makes a long tube down inside the flower and delivers material called sperm. Sperm combines with the ovule, and that's called fertilization."

"And that's what makes the ovule grow into a seed, and the seed can grow into a new plant? So are the new plants the children of the mother that made the egg and the father that made the pollen?"

"Exactly so," the Elf confirmed. "But I have another question. Why do you think these flowers need help from insects to spread pollen to other plants?"

"I guess it's because plants are stuck in one place and can't move around like animals," said Varun.

"That's very good thinking," said Aubrey. "But pine trees and grasses make a lot of pollen, and they just let the wind blow it."

"I bet if the wind has to blow it, a lot gets lost. So those plants have to make a lot of extra pollen," said Varun.

"Congratulations! You are a clever fellow."

Varun was pleased by the Elf's complement. "I think with bees and flowers it's sort of a trade, isn't it? The plant makes nectar so the bees will

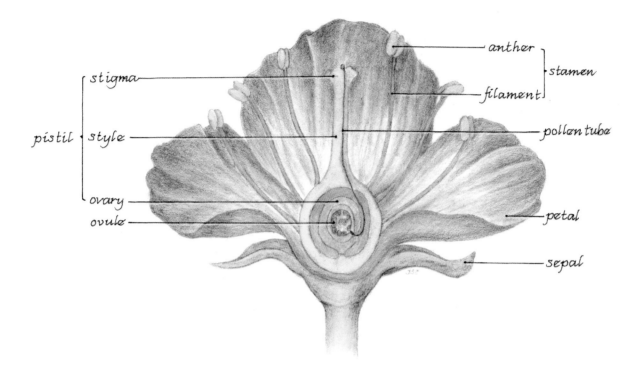

stigma

pistil

style

ovary

ovule

anther

stamen

filament

pollen tube

petal

sepal

The flower in this picture is sliced open so you can see what is inside. Varun was sitting on a petal when Lizzy arrived. The pollen is in the anthers at the ends of the stamens. Lizzy was dusted with pollen when she brushed against the anthers. You can see how pollen that is brought to a flower and lands on the stigma grows a long tube down into the ovary to find the ovules. Sometimes flowers can pollinate themselves, but the system works best when the pollen is taken to another flower.

come, and the bees carry pollen for the plant. But the bees also snitch some of the pollen for themselves, because they like to eat it."

"They do indeed," said the Elf. He slapped his forehead: "What kind of a host am I? You haven't had any food since you arrived on my doorstep. Would you like something to eat?"

In the excitement of the morning, Varun had totally forgotten about eating, but the Elf's words were now welcome. "That would be great. I don't remember eating breakfast, and I'm hungry."

"Well then, time for lunch," said Aubrey. "But we need to get back on the ground first."

CHAPTER 7

The Scarlet Sage and a Deepening Mystery

Varun and the Elf started to climb down their respective stems, but when Varun had descended about a quarter of the way, his feet slipped off the base of a leaf, and he fell. To his great relief he landed lightly on some dead leaves. He picked himself up with only wounded pride and a small scratch on one arm.

"There are some advantages to being very small," said Aubrey. "Being so light, you don't land hard. That's physics. Here, take my hand."

As Varun felt Aubrey's grasp his surroundings started to shrink, or perhaps he was growing? It was over in an instant, and he was standing next to the Elf, both restored to normal size.

"How did you do that?" Varun exclaimed. He was struggling to believe that his visit with the bee had really happened.

The Elf just smiled and began to walk toward the cottage. "Come. Let's have some lunch."

They made their way to the back of the cottage where there was a little stone terrace with a green table and matching wooden chairs. An old apple tree, now heavy with fruit, grew at the edge of the terrace. Next to the terrace was a small area with a circle of rocks around it and a little sign reading "Herb Garden." Varun looked at the labels on the plants. Many of the words were strange—basil, chives, dill, marjoram, oregano, savory, and thyme—but a couple seemed familiar. "Aren't those things Mom puts in food?" he asked.

"That's right. All of these plants are used to make food taste more interesting. Most people buy herbs and spices at the store in little bags or cans. They have no idea where they came from," said the Elf. "But as you have noticed them, I have a question for you. Why do you think plants go to the trouble of making spices?"

Varun remembered their conversation about why plants make colored flowers and why the flowers make nectar. "I guess it's because spices must do something for the plants, but I can't think what it is."

"Have you ever considered emptying the contents of the pepper shaker onto your plate and eating it?"

"Of course not! That would be yucky!"

"It certainly would warm up your mouth," agreed the Elf. "A lot of any spice can be too much of a good thing. Even very unpleasant."

"Do you mean those plants try to keep animals from eating them by tasting bad?" said Varun.

"Exactly so. All of these plants are simply defending themselves, and some of them are actually poisonous to small animals."

The scratch on his arm was itching, and as he reached to scratch it, Varun had another thought. "I think having thorns must be sort of like tasting bad. Prickles would be hard to eat too."

"That's a good comparison," Aubrey agreed.

One plant, with a long stalk of bright red, tubular flowers, stood out from all the others growing next to the house. It so caught Varun's attention that he read the label aloud: "Scarlet Sage."

"That plant is called a sage because it is wise and gives good advice," Aubrey explained.

"I think that's silly. Plants can't talk or give advice." At moments like this, the Elf reminded Varun of his Grandfather.

"Well, think what you will. That is an astute and sagacious plant."

Varun was not sure what astute and sagacious meant and whether the Elf was teasing him or getting philosophical again. He decided to think about it and not say anything. Little did he realize he had not heard the last of the Scarlet Sage.

"Wait here. I'm going to get our lunch," Aubrey called over his shoulder as he disappeared into the cottage.

Varun took a seat on the bench and had scarcely wondered what the apples on the tree might taste like when the Elf returned with a tray. Lunch consisted of peanut butter and jelly sandwiches, milk, and chocolate-chip cookies. Varun decided Aubrey was particularly fond of peanut butter and jelly sandwiches because he ate three of them. They each had an apple from the tree, and Varun thought his was the best apple he had ever tasted. Some

wasps had begun to gather at the jelly drippings, but Aubrey whispered to them, and they promptly flew away.

The Elf seemed more mysterious with each passing moment, and Varun thought about the red flower again.

"Were you kidding me about the Scarlet Sage?" he asked. Ordinarily he would have thought that question was too dumb to ask, but everything about the Elf was puzzling, and like his experiences with the bat and the bee, hard to accept as real.

Aubrey stood up, stretched, and ignored Varun's question. "I think the questing game is going pretty well, don't you?"

"I don't really understand what you mean by questing game." Varun pleaded.

"Are you having fun?"

Varun hesitated. "I guess so."

Aubrey looked at him without speaking.

"Well, William and Lizzy were a lot of fun to meet," said Varun. "But sometimes when I ask you something, you only ask another question about something else."

"That's part of the game," was Aubrey's cheerful response. "Have you discovered anything?"

Varun gave up. "Well, I've discovered interesting things about bats, and bees, and some other stuff. And I've discovered that sometimes you're hard to talk to."

The Elf smiled. "Have you discovered anything about yourself?"

This question puzzled Varun. "I don't know," he said finally.

Aubrey put his hand on Varun's shoulder. "If I'm not mistaken, you would like very much to visit the bees in their home. Let's go."

As they left the terrace, Varun thought about the Elf's words, but he couldn't make heads or tails of them. He still had no idea where he was, or even why, but surprisingly this didn't seem to matter. He was having a good time, and Aubrey was proving to be an interesting, if sometimes frustrating, companion. But a quest? What did that mean? And what about the Scarlet Sage? And what had really happened in the garden? How could Aubrey have reduced them both to the size of a honey bee? The memory was clear: he was sure he had really stood next to a bee named Lizzy while she told him about her antennae, compound eyes, and collecting pollen!

Together they followed a narrow path across a meadow. The land sloped upward, and the path began to wind back and forth, making the climb easier. Grasshoppers leapt out of the grass on either side as they passed, and at one point a rabbit bounded across the path. As they climbed higher, Varun started to pant. The Elf seemed to be extraordinarily agile, and Varun was on the verge of asking if they could rest when Aubrey stopped.

"We're almost there. We'll wait here a moment and listen to the music."

Varun could see the edge of a wood ahead, and while he stood quietly, catching his breath, he heard it. "Is someone trying to play a flute?"

"That's a Wood Thrush. He's a distant relative of robins."

"This seems like magic," said Varun.

"Well it isn't really magic. Remember, our game has rules. The second rule is: You can hear a lot just by listening."

Varun laughed. "You made up that rule right now, didn't you? It sounds like more of what you call philosophy!"

"There you go! But these rules of the game are how you get the world to bring you its 'magic.'"

CHAPTER 8

Dancing Bees

At last, Varun and the Elf the reached the top of the ridge. A low stone wall separated the meadow behind them from woodland ahead. They turned and gazed at the distant hills and listened to the thrush.

"Caught your breath now?"

Varun nodded.

"Come," said Aubrey. He stepped over the old stone wall and led Varun a short way into the woods. They stopped near an ancient tree, and Aubrey pointed to a small hole near the base of the trunk. Varun looked down. He could see bees busily going in and out from a landing spot at the opening.

"Would you like to go inside and see how the bees live?" Aubrey asked.

That had seemed a good plan when they had been at the Elf's cottage, but now Varun was remembering that bees will sting if you bother them. With so many bees around, the prospect of becoming small and going into their house suddenly made him very nervous. "Is it really safe?" he asked.

"You will be completely safe with me," Aubrey reassured him. "Here, take my hand."

Varun slowly offered his palm, and once again he had the feeling that everything around him was growing. This time, however, he was not so startled to find himself scarcely larger than the bees coming and going through the hole. But being so small still made him feel very vulnerable.

"Come with me, stay close, and you'll be okay." Aubrey sounded confident, but Varun was still not sure. He didn't want to be stung when he was his full size, and he was certain it would be awful in his present state.

Several bees that were standing around the entrance suddenly leaned forward, thrust the back end of their abdomens up in the air, and fanned their wings. Varun thought he smelled something that had not been present before. A rush of angry bees poured from the hive, looking around for trouble. Varun tried to get behind the Elf and make himself even smaller.

"Calm down, Harriet. It's me, Aubrey."

"Oh, it's only you," said the nearest fanning bee in a small irritated buzz. She lowered her abdomen, and the other bees followed her lead. Soon the general buzzing and flying about stopped, calm returned to the hive, and all the bees went back to what they had been doing before their visitors arrived.

"Why did they do that?" asked Varun, still feeling nervous.

"Those bees fanning their wings are guard bees. They make an odor

from glands in their abdomen and spread it around by fanning the air," said the Elf.

"That smell must be like an alarm bell", said Varun. "The bees that rushed outside looked like they were ready to attack."

"They were. Many creatures, from mice to bears and even other bees, would like to steal their honey."

"Are you sure they won't mind if we go inside?"

"It will be alright. But on this visit we are not going to interrupt them. We are only going to watch."

"You mean we can't talk to them?"

Varun's encounter with Lizzy had been fun, and the Elf saw Varun's disappointment. "It's part of our game of discovery. You will find some of the bees behaving in strange ways, and your challenge is to figure out what they are doing."

Varun's forehead wrinkled. "I don't get it."

"You will, quickly enough," Aubrey offered in encouragement. "Remember the first rule of the quest: you can see a lot just by looking. Now, follow me."

As soon as they had passed through the narrow entrance, the light was dim, and Varun could barely make out honeycombs deeper in the hive. "It smells funny in here," he announced.

"That's the smell of a beehive," said the Elf. "One reason is this gum-my stuff. It's called propolis, and the bees make it from saps and resins they collect from plants."

"What do they do with it?"

"They fill cracks with it, and it kills germs. Each bee has the odor of her own hive, and that helps the guard bees recognize strangers."

As Varun's eyes adjusted to the dim light, he saw three bees that had attracted the attention of other bees. Each of the three walked forward several steps while wagging her abdomen from side to side. Then she stopped wagging, walked in a half circle back to where she had started, and repeated the waggle-walk forward along the same path.

This performance stirred Varun's curiosity, and he forgot his fear of being stung. "What are they doing?" he asked.

"People call that a bee-dance, maybe because it reminds them of what they do when they square-dance."

"Do bees dance for fun?"

"There is a purpose to the dance. Remember what I said about being a good observer? Watch them for a few minutes, and then tell me what else you see."

Varun concluded he was not going to get his question answered unless he played by the Elf's rules, so he looked more closely at the three dancing bees.

"Two of them are waggle-walking in the same direction. The other one is wagglewalking in a different direction, and he is not dancing nearly as fast."

"She is not dancing as fast," Aubrey corrected. "All the bees you see now are females."

"But Lizzy said she had some brothers?"

"That's right, but they look different. We will meet them later. For now I want to know what else you are seeing. What about the other bees that are gathered around the dancers?"

Varun turned his attention to those bees. "They get close to the dancer, and they touch her with their antennae. There is a group around her all the time, but no bee stays close to her for long. When a bee leaves the group, it goes outside. When they go outside, I don't see them come back, so maybe they fly off somewhere."

"That's good. Very good indeed," approved the Elf. "You have now seen most of the pieces of the puzzle of why bees dance. Can you put the pieces together?"

Varun was confused. "I don't get it."

"Here's a clue. What direction are the two fast waggle-dancers going when they do the waggle-walk part of the dance?"

Varun wondered for a moment what that direction might mean. Then he thought he knew. "That's the direction you and I came from. Down the hill!"

"And what's at the bottom of the hill?"

"I get it. The garden! With the flowers! The dancers must be telling the other bees the direction to fly to find flowers. And I'll bet the bees that leave the dancers and go outside are flying to the garden." He thought for a moment. "Do you think that when they touch the dancer with their antennae they can smell the kind of flower she was visiting?"

"That's a good bet," agreed Aubrey. "And if you were in the garden right now, the same bees that you have seen here following the dancers would be arriving at the flowers. Now look at the third dancer, the slow one. As you observed, she is dancing in another direction."

"That must mean she has found flowers somewhere else, in that direction." Varun was beginning to be enthusiastic about the Elf's idea of fun.

"Ah, but why is she dancing slower?" Aubrey asked.

"I don't know."

"Can you guess?"

"Well maybe she is not as excited about the flowers she has found."

"Good guess, and almost right. If you followed her directions and found the flowers, you would discover that they are farther away than my garden."

"You mean the faster the waggle-run is repeated, the closer are the flowers?"

The Elf nodded.

"I guess it does make sense for the dance to be faster when the flowers are close. The bees ought to be more excited if they don't have to fly far," said Varun. He thought for a few moments. "So by following the dance for only a few waggle-runs, a bee finds out two things. She learns the direction she has to fly to find the flowers, and how far she has to fly. And when she gets close, she smells the flowers and sees them, just like Lizzy told me."

"That's what I call a great discovery," said Aubrey, "and you did a good job of figuring it out with only a little help from me."

The Elf's words made Varun feel proud, and he imagined the foragers arriving in Aubrey's garden and finding the right plants to visit.

"Is all nectar the same?" he asked. He liked to eat some things better than others, and he thought maybe bees did too.

"Some flowers have sweeter nectar than others, and these are the better flowers from which to collect. The dance also tells the bees about the sweetness of the nectar. Can you guess how it does that?"

Varun thought for a few moments, but he couldn't see how. "I give up. Tell me."

"I will, because you would have to watch the dances for a long time to get the answer. But it is really very simple. The sweeter the nectar, the longer a bee dances."

Varun saw a problem. "But the bees don't stay with a dancer for more than a few waggle-runs. So they can't know anything about how sweet the nectar is."

"Congratulations, Varun. That is absolutely right. You may grow up to be a detective or a scientist. Maybe even a philosopher. But think about this. What do you suppose happens when a bee dances for a long time?"

Varun considered this for a moment. "Oh, I see. The longer a dance goes on, the more bees are directed to the flowers. That means if the nectar is especially sweet, more bees will go look for it, and more nectar will be brought back to the hive. That's pretty clever!"

"Flowers that attract bees and dust them with pollen also seem clever," said Aubrey.

"Flowers can't be clever. Plants don't have brains to think with."

"Ahh," said the Elf. "Much about plants and animals seems clever because it serves a useful purpose for them, but that does not mean those plants and animals are intelligent. Bees don't think about things the way you do."

Varun had never considered this idea. Bees and flowers do things that have a purpose and are useful, but they don't think or plan! This was a very complicated idea, and Varun decided he would ask about it later, when there was not so much happening.

"There's another example to think about right behind you," said Aubrey.

Varun turned around. A bee was dancing, but not like the other bees he had seen. She ran in a small circle, then turned and ran back around the circle the other way. Observer bees followed her closely, touching her with their antennae as she repeated her dance.

Varun laughed. "She doesn't seem to know where the flowers are. She isn't pointing anywhere. Is she confused?"

"No, she's not confused. That's called a round dance. Her dance means that the flowers are nearby. Most likely they're at the edge of the meadow where it meets the woods."

"Then the collecting bees must have to find the flowers by smell?" said Varun.

"That's right," agreed Aubrey. "They search around the hive until they find them. But when they go back for a second load of nectar, they remember where the flowers are and go directly to them."

"So bees have memories too?"

The Elf nodded. "You have made several important discoveries about bees this afternoon, but before we leave the hive, there are still a couple of surprises waiting for you. They are even more amazing than what you have seen so far, but for this we have to go deeper into the hive, into total darkness."

CHAPTER 9

Codes and Clocks in the Darkness of the Hive

Varun felt pleased he had figured out how a bee tells other bees how to find a source of nectar, but he was not sure he wanted to go farther into the hive.

"You said it's dark in there. We won't be able to see anything." The Elf took an object from his pocket and held it in his open palm.

"That looks like a seed from your garden," Varun said.

Aubrey rubbed the seed with his handkerchief, and to Varun's astonishment, the seed began to cast a light from one end.

"How did you do that? It's like a little flashlight."

"Plants capture sunlight and store it. That's what makes them grow. We Elves know how to get light back out of seeds."

Varun found this interesting, but he was suspicious Aubrey was teasing him. "Do only Elves know how to get light out of plants?"

"What do you think happens when wood burns?"

"That's different. The wood gets hot and burns up."

"You burn food to get energy for your muscles. You just do it so slowly you don't get hot and glow in the dark. Do you know what a firefly is?"

"Are they the same thing as lightning bugs?"

"You've got it. But they are neither flies nor bugs; they are really beetles."

"Oh, I've seen them. In the summer they come out when it begins to get dark. They don't fly fast, and if you are quick, you can catch them in your hand. They have a flashing light in their rear end, and it's not hot." Varun paused, remembering the fun. "But why do they flash like that?"

"It's sort of flirting. The males flash to get the attention of females, and the females flash back to show where they are. And different colors announce what kind of firefly they are. But enough of this. Come. We have things to see here. Follow me."

Aubrey led the way deeper into the hive, and soon the only light was from his tiny seed flashlight. The odor of propolis intensified and mingled with the smells of beeswax and honey. The hive was nearly filled with slabs of wax honeycomb hanging from the top of the cavity in the tree. Bees crawled on the combs, but Aubrey and Varun made their way through the spaces between combs. Varun could hear the gentle stirring of bees all around him, going about their various tasks.

"The honey is made over there, but what I want you to see now is right here, still not far from the entrance." The Elf directed a spot of light onto a comb, and Varun could see a bee waggle-dancing on the surface.

"What is she doing up there?" Varun laughed. "How can she tell those other bees which direction to fly by dancing on the wall?"

"Most of the dancing is done up there, not on the flat where you first saw it. The message is the same, but here the dance is in code."

"A code? A secret code?" Varun found that idea exciting.

"It's a simple code. It has to do with where the sun is outside the hive."

"What do you mean?"

"Now listen carefully. Imagine there is a clock on that wall. The number 12 is at the top, the 6 is at the bottom, and the bee is dancing right in the middle. Suppose the waggle-walk is straight up the wall, toward the 12. That means fly in the direction of the sun to find the flowers."

"You mean fly up in the air toward the sun? There aren't any flowers up there."

"Of course not. It means fly several feet off the ground, but keep the sun in front of you. And if the dance is directed straight down, toward the imaginary 6, it means keep the sun behind you while flying to the flowers."

"I think I get it. That bee is waggle-walking to one side, towards where 9 o'clock would be. That means when its followers fly to find the flowers, they will keep the sun on their right."

"And," said Aubrey, "if you were a bee, doing a waggle-walk towards the 4 on the clock, where would the sun be as you flew toward the flowers?"

Varun imagined a bee doing a waggle-walk towards 4 on the imaginary clock, and he saw it in his mind's eye something like this:

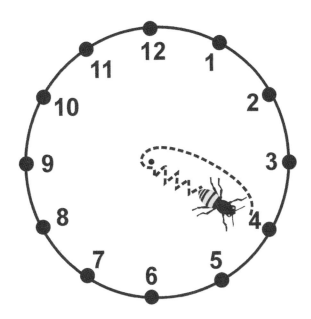

After each waggle-walk, the imagined bee came straight back to the center of the clock and waggle-walked to the 4 again. "The sun is on my left side and behind me, like this" Varun tried a waggle-walk of his own, stretching out his left arm and pointing to the rear and towards where the 12 would be. He promptly tripped over a passing bee. The bee didn't stop, but Varun thought he heard it mutter something about a clumsy drone being in everybody's way.

"Oh, I'm sorry!" said Varun, but the bee was gone. "I've forgotten. What's a drone?"

"One of the brothers. We won't see them today. Before we go, however, you have one more thing to discover about the dances. I think you will find it even more surprising than the code."

"What's that?"

"Suppose you are a bee dancing towards the 4 on the clock. You have found especially sweet nectar, so you keep dancing for several hours. Do you think your dance will still show the right direction?"

"What do you mean?"

"Does the sun stand still in the sky?"

"No, the sun moves across the sky during the day." As he spoke, Varun quickly understood the connection. "Oh, I see. After several hours, the sun will have moved, and the dance should be pointing to a different time on the pretend clock. Now when the follower bees go outside, they will have a hard time finding the flowers." Varun was pleased to have figured that out.

"So you would expect," agreed Aubrey. "But it doesn't happen. When a bee dances for a long time, she gradually shifts the direction of her waggle-run to correct for the slow movement of the sun in the sky. Her directions to the other bees remain correct."

"Bees don't wear watches," said Varun. "How do they know the time?"

"They have a very good sense of time. They have an internal clock."

"Is that really true?"

"It's really true. I said you would be amazed. But now we have to go. My sense of time tells me it's getting late."

The Elf led the way back to the entrance. "You have discovered an astonishing amount about the dances of bees. They don't talk among themselves as we do, but they communicate with each other about things that are important to them."

"But Lizzy talked to me, and that bee I accidentally kicked also talked, and so did William. I heard them."

"Remember, you can only hear those voices when an Elf is with you. What I show you, however, you can see for yourself, even without me."

This seemed strange to Varun, but then he had never known an Elf before. Maybe that is just the way Elves are, he decided.

As they emerged from the hive into the late afternoon sunlight, Varun realized he had missed one of the things he had wanted to see. "You didn't show me the drones," he protested.

"Indeed. There are many things you have yet to see. But there will be time before you go home. Right now we need to think about dinner."

Aubrey took Varun by the hand, and the world around them began to shrink. Varun shot up out of grass as it fell away under his feet, and in an instant he had regained his normal size.

"It will be very much faster to walk back this way, and I don't want you to meet a shrew when you are the size of an insect. They know better than to mess with an Elf, but it could be a bad experience for you if they thought you were alone"

"What's a shrew?"

"A shrew is the size of a small mouse. It has hair like a mouse, but it has sharp, pointed teeth. It eats worms and insects. It is one of the reasons you must keep close to me when you are tiny."

Varun shuddered. Yes, if he met a shrew while he was the size of an insect it would be like meeting a tiger on any other day. He was glad to be his own size again for the walk back.

The sun was setting over the ridge to the west when they reached the cottage, and Varun was feeling tired and hungry. Although the day had been sunny and warm, the evening began to get chilly. Aubrey started a fire in the fireplace, and the warmth in the room made Varun sleepy. The Elf produced two bowls of stew and some bread and butter as if from nowhere, and before he had finished his, Varun's head began to nod. Aubrey showed him to a tiny bedroom, and Varun fell quickly into a bed with a thick, fluffy quilt filled with goose down. He was asleep as his head found the pillow.

CHAPTER 10

Varun Does an Experiment

Varun awoke as the first rays of the morning sun came through the window. He crawled out from under the covers and sat on the edge of the bed, listening to a song sparrow and a Carolina wren. He wondered what they were and if they were competing to see who could greet the day most enthusiastically. When he looked out the window he decided the one with the turned-up tail, longer bill, and bigger voice, was the winner.

When he had rubbed the remaining cobwebs from his sleepy eyes, he spotted an envelope lying on the end of the table under the window. To his surprise, it was addressed to him. In the upper left corner of the envelope, where the return address should be, were the initials S.S. He opened the envelope and pulled out a hand-written letter in elegant, flowing script and began to read.

Sunrise, This Morning
Master Varun
The Elf's Cottage

Dear Varun,

Greetings and salutations. We are most happy to have you with us for a few days and are pleased that you are quickly discovering how to be a careful observer of the world. Not everyone is a careful observer.

In a few days you will be going home, and I hope you will remember what you are discovering while you are here. The most important lesson is that things are not always what they seem to be. Being a careful observer is the first step in finding out how things really are, rather than how you imagine them to be, or how you wish they might be. The second step is to ask questions. Never be afraid to ask questions.

As you grow up you will be surprised to find how many people have not mastered these skills. The Elf is an excellent instructor and enjoys answering questions. (Well, most of the time.) When you get home you will find the things he is showing you are not make-believe. Bees dance for the same reasons that you have observed and figured out.

There is mystery about the Elf, as there is about much of the world, but think of him as a guide, leading you into unknown territory on your quest. When he leaves you, as he will when you go home, you will know much more about being your own guide on future expeditions.

Sagaciously yours,
The Scarlet Sage

Varun put the letter next to the envelope and thought about it. Aubrey had said the Scarlet Sage gave good advice. Had that plant really written him a letter? Strange things happened when he was around Aubrey, but maybe this was the Elf's way of getting him to see better what was really real. His thoughts were suddenly interrupted by Aubrey's voice from the other room.

"I hear you're up and ready for another adventure, and breakfast is ready for you! Wasn't the singing of those two birds grand? I particularly like the Carolina wren."

"I heard it, and I saw it too. It was right outside the window. Is it the one with the turned-up tail? It's really loud for such a little bird."

"It is indeed," said Aubrey. "Now let's eat. It's a new day."

While they were having breakfast of oatmeal with toast and honey, orange juice, and milk, Varun asked what they were going to do next.

"Ahh," said Aubrey, "we're going to do an experiment."

"What sort of experiment?"

"You'll find out after breakfast."

Varun set about eating as fast as he could. As soon as they were through they cleaned the dishes. This did not take more than a few moments. Everything the Elf did in the kitchen seemed to be finished as soon as he began. Then Aubrey got a little cart out of a shed behind the cottage and loaded it with a small folding table, two folding stools like the ones in his garden, and a box with a lid. Then he added the knapsack with their lunch.

Varun motioned toward the box. "What's in there?"

Aubrey continued to be mysterious. "It's about asking questions and getting answers. Let's go." He pulled the cart around to the front of the cottage, through the gate in the picket fence, and started down the road with Varun at his side.

When they came to a place where there were no flowers blooming, the Elf pulled the cart into a grassy area at the side of the road and set up the table and the stools. Then he opened the box, took out a large piece of blue paper cut in the shape of a round flower, and put it on the table. He placed a small, shallow dish in the center of the flower and filled it with a clear liquid from a bottle in the box.

"What's that?" said Varun, unable to contain his curiosity any longer.

"Taste it."

Varun dipped a finger and licked it. "It's sweet; it must be sugar water."

"It has a lot of sugar in it, so the bees will be quite interested to find it."

Aubrey added three small bottles of colored paint and three tiny brushes to the other things he had put on the table.

"Now let's wait." He sat on one of the folding stools and pointed to the other for Varun to sit.

"What are we waiting for?"

"We are offering bees a sweet drink at this artificial flower. We can make it seem more real to them, though." He took another bottle out of the box and placed a few drops of another liquid on the paper next to the dish.

"Peppermint oil; take a sniff," he said.

"Wow. That sure makes it smell like a flower! But how will the bees find it? There aren't any flowers anywhere around here."

"Most flowers don't bloom for long, so there are always scout bees searching for new sources of nectar. As you learned from Lizzy, bees have a keen sense of smell. Scouts will likely smell this on the breeze long before they see it."

"But what is the experiment?"

"Do you remember yesterday, when you saw bees leaving the dancers, you decided they were going to my garden?"

"Yes, and you said that if we were in the garden we would see them arrive."

"Ahh, but how would we know they were the same bees?"

Varun thought about that for a second. "You could ask them."

"Perhaps. But how could you ask the same question and get an answer?"

Varun was puzzled. The bees all looked alike, and without the Elf being there he certainly couldn't speak to them. "I don't know. Is there a way?"

"That's what an experiment is. It's a way of asking a question of Mother Nature and getting an answer. And the experiment we are doing today is to answer a question much like the one I asked a minute ago."

As Aubrey was talking, a bee landed on the paper flower and walked to the edge of the dish. It stuck its mouthparts into the sugar syrup and began to drink. The Elf quickly picked up one of the little paint brushes and dabbed a tiny red spot in the middle of the bee's back.

Varun was excited. "I get it! You marked that bee so that it will be different from all the others."

"And what do you expect that bee to do?"

"It is going to go back to the hive, and if it likes what you put in that dish, it will dance. And the dance will point in this direction."

"That's a hypothesis," said Aubrey.

"Is a hypothesis philosophy?" Varun was not sure he liked the direction the conversation was headed now.

"Think of it as a prediction. In this case, it's a prediction about why bees dance. And it is a prediction that can be tested by the experiment we are now doing. All we have to do is go back to the hive and see if this bee is pointing its dance in this direction. But let's wait until a few more bees have found this flower."

When the Elf had marked another bee with yellow paint and Varun had marked a third one with blue, they left the table and started to walk straight as the crow flies toward the bee tree they had visited the day before.

"Now," said Aubrey, "turn and face the sun."

When Varun was facing in the direction of the sun, Aubrey said "Imagine you are standing in the center of a clock face looking at the number 12."

Varun saw right away what was coming next. He pointed with left arm in the direction from which they had come. "The dances should be pointing toward the number 10 on the pretend clock," he exclaimed.

"Why do you say that?"

"Because if I were a bee flying in that direction I would get to the table with the flower, like this…" Varun turned to face in the direction he had been pointing and flapped his arms as though he were flying. "…then the sun would be over here." He pointed his right arm in the direction of the sun.

"Let's see if they are dancing as you predict. Are you ready?"

Varun could hardly wait to find the bees with the spots of paint, and he grasped the Elf's outstretched hand. Once again there was a disconcerting sensation as the world around him expanded and he found himself at the entrance to the hive, very much smaller than he had just been. Harriet was on guard duty at the entrance, but this time she paid no attention to them as they entered.

"We must smell like we belong in this hive," said Varun. "The guard bees don't seem to care like they did when we came yesterday."

"Another good observation," said Aubrey. "But remember, when we go inside we are still observers. We will simply watch the bees and not interrupt what they are doing until our experiment is finished."

There were no bees with painted spots dancing on the level area near the entrance. Varun was not disappointed because he remembered that most of the dances are done on the vertical sides of combs. The Elf took one of the seeds he kept in his pocket and lighted the way deeper into the hive.

There were six bees dancing on the side of the same comb, eagerly followed by other bees. To Varun's delight, two were marked with paint, one red and the other blue that he had put on. During the waggle part of their dance, both of the marked bees were walking toward the 10 on an imaginary clock.

"That is the coolest thing yet," Varun exclaimed with joy.

"You have now done an experiment that confirms the meaning of the dances. You predicted the direction of the dances that would be done by the marked bees. Then you came to the hive and found the marked bees dancing as you predicted. Your experiment was similar to the many experiments done by the scientists who discovered the meaning of the bees' dances."

"Are you telling me that an experiment is a way to ask bees something, and then find out what they would say if they could talk to you?"

"Experiments are not just for talking to bees. If you know the right questions to ask, you can communicate with birds, and flowers, and everything else in the world, even rocks or stars. The hard part is figuring out how to ask the right question so you get an answer that tells you exactly what you want to know."

Varun thought the Elf was sounding philosophical again, but he was beginning to understand something that seemed pretty important. Maybe there were ways to find out things that even Elves didn't know! If you could ask the right question, nature would give you the answer.

Aubrey seemed to be reading his mind. "You are a clever boy. But you've only met Lizzy and Harriet. How would like to meet some of the other bees?"

"Oh, yes. That would be fun. Let's do it."

CHAPTER 11

A Visit to the Nursery

Varun felt pleased with himself. He and the Elf had played a game to solve a mystery. Aubrey said games like that are called experiments, and experiments answer questions that you can't ask another person or look up in books. He felt proud to have done an experiment just like one that scientists did when they first decoded the dances of honeybees. But right now he was keen to meet more bees and find out what else they do.

They made their way deeper into the hive, and Varun found himself wrapped again in its now familiar smells of honey, propolis, and beeswax.

Aubrey spoke to a passing bee. "Do you know where the queen is this morning?"

"How should I know?" whined the bee. "All I do is clean up after everyone else." The bee hurried on toward the entrance, carrying some trash.

"That's Martha," Aubrey explained. "She's still young. There are many jobs to do in the hive, and house cleaning is done by the youngest bees. She will feel better as soon as she is old enough to feed the larvae."

"What do baby bees look like?"

"You mean larvae," Aubrey reminded him. "You will see at the next comb."

The Elf turned up the light on his seed flashlight, and they walked deeper into the darkness of the hive. Varun noticed that some of the cells on the next comb were open, whereas others were closed with wax caps.

Aubrey motioned to a bee. "Nicole, could Varun see some of the larvae in your care."

"Go right ahead," said Nicole with a touch of pride. "I've just finished feeding them an early lunch."

Aubrey pointed his light into one of the open cells, and Varun saw what looked like a tiny grain of rice on the bottom.

"That's an egg," explained Nicole.

It didn't look like much to Varun. "What's inside?" he asked.

"Look in this cell," Nicole suggested.

The Elf brought the light closer, and when Varun peered inside the cell, he saw a tiny worm-like creature curled up at the bottom.

"That's what they look like when the egg hatches. We feed them honey and pollen and they grow," Nicole explained. She showed him two more cells, each with a larger larva inside.

"Don't they ever come out?"

"Not looking like that. After about 12 days they are so big they almost fill the cell. Then we put a wax cap on top, and inside they begin to turn into

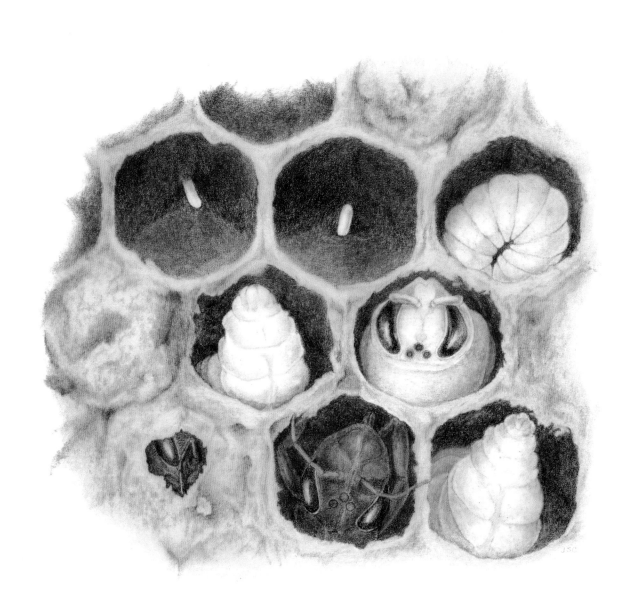

adult bees. After another 12 days they chew the cap off and come out looking like me. Come, I'll show you."

The cells on the next comb all had wax caps, but with the light shining on them, Varun could make out something dark inside. "I get it," he exclaimed. "They are like caterpillars — except they don't crawl around on plants eating leaves. They stay inside the comb and get fed. That seems sort of lazy. Then you put lids on the cells, and the larvae turn into, I forget. What do you call them?"

"Pupae," Aubrey reminded him.

"They turn into pupae and change their shape, and grow wings and legs and eyes. Sort of like butterflies," Varun exclaimed.

"You've got it," said Aubrey. Then turning to Nicole he asked if she knew where they could find the queen.

Nicole pointed. "I think you will find her about three combs that way. That's where we are expanding the nursery. The hive is beginning to get crowded."

"Thanks for showing me the larvae," said Varun. "You seem to like to take care of them."

"Oh, I do! But I'm looking forward to going outside and visiting flowers. That will be really nice, but the most fun will be when I can dance every day."

Aubrey departed in search of the queen, but to his dismay Varun couldn't lift his feet. His shoes seemed to be nailed to the floor. "Aubrey, wait," he said, just as the Elf disappeared around the end of the comb, leaving him in total darkness. He panicked. "Aubrey! Help! Come back! I'm stuck!"

To his great relief, the light was not long in returning, and with the Elf right behind it.

"I see you've managed to stand in some fresh propolis. It's pretty good glue, isn't it?" The Elf summoned a couple of passing bees, and they set about removing the gum from Varun's shoes by chewing it off.

"They can do a lot with their mouths," Aubrey observed. "As soon as you can move your feet, let's find the queen."

They had scarcely gotten under way again when Varun was startled by a group of large bees whose enormous eyes covered most of their heads. He grabbed the Elf's arm and whispered "Who are they? Are they queens?"

"No. There is only one queen in the hive. These are drones; they are the brothers of the worker bees."

The drones seemed to be sleeping. A few were awake, but unlike most of the bees that Varun had encountered so far, they were not doing anything useful. Varun thought he heard one of them hail a passing bee: "You, Kelsey, how about bringing me some honey; I'm hungry," and Kelsey responding: "You're a lazy good-for-nothing, Duane. Why don't you try to get it for yourself?"

Duane, who had been cleaning his antennae with his front legs, apparently decided he was not so hungry after all. He settled down and began to doze.

"Why are their eyes so big?" asked Varun.

"The drones have only one job to do. They don't collect nectar. They don't make honey or make wax combs, and they don't take care of the young or clean the hive."

"What do they do?"

"Do you remember in the garden how we saw bees and butterflies getting dusted with pollen when they fed from flowers?"

"Yes. And when they pollinated another plant, it could make seeds and new plants."

"That's right," said Aubrey, "but pollen is only for plants. Male bees and other male animals deliver their sperm themselves."

Varun was getting impatient with the Elf's meandering answer. "What does this have to do with drones' big eyes?"

"I'm getting to that. Be patient. Drones have to deliver sperm to a queen before she can lay fertilized eggs. That happens when a new queen is about to take over a hive. The reason a drone's eyes are so big is that he has to find a new queen from some other hive while she is flying around and then give her some sperm. She keeps the sperm in a little pouch inside her abdomen. In fact she gets sperm from about a dozen drones before she comes back to the hive to lay eggs."

"Is that *really* all drones do?" Varun didn't think just handing out sperm to young queens made for a very exciting life.

"That's all, and that is why there are thousands of worker bees in the hive, all sisters and doing all the work, but only a few hundred drones at most."

"I heard Duane trying to get one of his sisters to wait on him and bring him food. It was funny," said Varun.

"If I had not been with you, there would have been nothing for you to hear," said Aubrey. "Remember, animals don't talk to each other like that. But what you think you heard tells you something about how the workers get along with their brothers. The drones can't even feed themselves; the workers have to feed them. If there are too many drones in the hive, the workers get fed up with them." The Elf chortled. "Get it? Fed up!"

That's another of his dumb jokes, Varun thought, and ignored it. "What happens then?"

"Oh that's good," said the Elf, wiping the tears from his eyes. "When they get fed up" — more laughing — "they make some of the drones go outside. That's very hard on the drones, because they can't take care of themselves. Although they are bigger than their sisters, they are quite helpless. They are also harmless. They don't sting. Now we still have to find the queen. Let's go. Fed up. I must remember that one."

Varun followed behind, pondering the strange nature of the bees' family: one mother, thousands of busy sisters, a bunch of brothers that didn't seem to be peppy or have much fun, and multiple fathers who had never been in the hive and were long since gone.

CHAPTER 12

An Inside-out World

At last Varun and the Elf found the new extension to the nursery. Comb was still under construction, and Varun could see bees building cells, using wax they secreted from under the scales on their abdomens. They measured the size of each new cell with their antennae.

Kelsey was one of the bees making new cells. "Notice how the cells have six sides," she said.

"That makes them hexagons," said Varun.

Kelsey ignored the interjection. "That means they pack together without any lost space," she said proudly. "That would also happen if they were squares or rectangles, but with six sides we can get even more cells on each comb and use less wax for each cell. And they are almost round, so there are no sharp corners inside."

"Who decides which bees do what job?" Varun asked.

"There's no boss. Not even the queen," said Aubrey. "In part it depends on how old the bees are. Martha is a young bee doing housecleaning. Nicole is a bit older and feeding the larvae. Most of the bees making wax comb are a bit older still, and the oldest ones are going outside to find nectar and pollen."

"But it doesn't always work that way," chimed in Kelsey. "If there is a need for one particular kind of work to be done, we bees do it. The hive needs more comb now, and I started making wax and building comb while I'm still young."

"Notice how she does it just as well as any other bee," said Aubrey.

"And no one told me how to do it!" said Kelsey, beaming with pride.

"Tomorrow you will see another way bees change jobs when there is need," Aubrey continued. "Now, let's find the queen."

Varun was very curious to see what the queen looked like. Their search ended at the far end of the comb, where there were newly finished cells. One bee was surrounded by a group of workers bringing her food and grooming her.

"There she is," said Aubrey.

Varun was surprised. The queen was not nearly as plump as the drones. She looked like a worker, except her body was longer, extending farther beyond the tips of her wings. She kept at her work, placing a single egg in the bottom of each empty cell until the Elf spoke to her.

"Hillary, this is Varun. He is finding out all about your offspring."

Hillary paused and turned to face them. "Hello, Aubrey. It's nice to see

you again. And Varun, it is a pleasure to have you visit. I'm sure Aubrey will show you everything, but do you have any questions for me?"

Varun thought for a moment. "Why do the boy bees look so different from the girl bees? They are bigger, and they have great big eyes and can't sting like their sisters."

The queen looked at the Elf, as if to ask where do I begin?

"He knows that you have a pouch of sperm to fertilize the eggs," said Aubrey.

"If I want the egg to hatch and grow up to be a daughter, I make sure that the egg is fertilized when I put it in an empty cell. But we bees and our neighbors the ants have a little trick. If we want a son, we don't fertilize the egg."

"That means the drones are not all here," Aubrey said with a chuckle.

"Hey, I thought eggs had to be fertilized in order to hatch and grow into new animals," said Varun.

"For most animals that is absolutely right. But bees and ants are different from most other animals," Aubrey explained.

Varun was still troubled. "Does this mean that I'm not all here?"

The Elf laughed. "Oh, no, only drones. Boys are all here. Sometimes boys behave as though they're not all here. But that's quite different."

"Well, back to the job. A queen's work is never done," said Hillary, who had already started to lay another egg.

"She almost never stops," said Aubrey. He started to lead the way back to the entrance of the hive, but as they came around the end of the next comb, he suddenly stopped. "Oh, here's a surprise for you."

Varun saw a group of cells that were larger than any he had seen before. They were closed, and their caps were rounded rather than flat like all the other cells he had seen. "What are these?" he asked. "They look like they have pupae inside."

"These are drone cells, and the drones are almost ready to come out. There is going to be some big excitement in a day or two."

But to Varun's question about what kind of excitement, the Elf would only say: "You'll see when the time comes."

When they got back outside and had been restored to their normal size, Varun spotted the Elf's knapsack hanging on a branch where they had left it. The sun had moved into the afternoon sky, and Varun's stomach told him they had stayed in the hive right through lunch-time.

Aubrey saw him looking wistfully at the knapsack. "Why don't we have a snack on the walk home," he said.

They started down the hill, chewing peanut butter and cucumber sandwiches. Varun found the combination surprisingly good, and said so.

"One of my favorites," Aubrey agreed, helping himself to another.

Varun decided this was the moment to ask the question he had been keeping since he arrived at the Elf's cottage. "Do you have any video games or stuff like that in your house?"

As so frequently happened, Aubrey responded with a question of his own. "Do you know what virtual reality is?"

"I think it's what you see when you play a game on the computer. You sit outside a pretend world and make things happen inside"

"That's a good example," said Aubrey. "During your visit with me, you have stepped inside a virtual reality, and you have become part of a game."

"You mean because you're an Elf, this place is a virtual reality?"

Aubrey nodded. "In our game, you are inside, looking out at your world and discovering things that you didn't see when you spent your time playing video games."

Varun grinned. "Hey, I'm in a sort of inside-out video game! It's fun!" He skipped ahead. "And I'm finding out all sorts of great stuff."

The idea of seeing the real world from a virtual reality was so new that Varun fell silent and began to think about other things that had happened while he was with Aubrey. The talking animals, his changes in size, the Elf himself, all seemed part of a virtual world. But hadn't the Scarlet Sage and Aubrey both told him he was discovering features of the real world? He puzzled about this paradox and the coming excitement for the rest of the day.

CHAPTER 13

Eight Legs and Eight Eyes

A t breakfast the next morning there was honey for the cereal and toast, and Varun began to wonder how honey was made, and how so many bees could live in such a small place. "That hive sure has a large amount of bees inside," he said.

"A large number of bees." said Aubrey.

"What's the difference?" Varun mumbled through a mouthful of honeyed-toast.

The Elf put down his spoon, leaned back in his chair, and cleared his throat. "The hive has a large amount of honey inside. But bees come as individuals that can be counted, and honey doesn't. So the hive has a large number of bees and a large amount of honey. That's the difference."

More mumbling. "I get it. There is a large amount of wax in the hive, and each honeycomb has a large number of cells in it"

"Right. And while we are on the subject, if a bear broke into the hive and made a big mess, the next day there would be less honey and fewer bees. Not fewer honey and less bees."

"Sometimes I think you sound just like my Grandpa," said Varun, having finally swallowed his toast. Then, ready to move on, he reminded Aubrey of the plan they had made the day before. "Are we really going to see the bees make honey today?"

"We are, but on the way I want you to see another of my friends."

As soon as they had tidied up from breakfast, they went to the little shed behind the cottage. The door was open, and a garden spider had built a large web in the opening. The spider was sitting in the center of the web, and the Elf greeted it as an old friend. "Good morning, Edith. I see you've been busy, but I thought you liked to spin your webs in the blueberry bushes."

"Ordinarily I do, but I hope you're not going to annoy me by knocking down this web. After all, you left the door open."

The Elf laughed. "Oh, no. Varun and I are going out, and I don't need anything in the shed today. You can keep your web, and maybe you will feel better if you can catch a fly for breakfast. Varun has a lot to discover while he is visiting us. Do you mind if he takes a close look at you? You are rather pretty."

Pacified by this attention, Edith stood on the tips of her legs to show off her bright yellow and black body.

"How many legs does Edith have?" Aubrey asked.

"Six," said Varun, but without bothering to count.

"I do not. I have eight. What do you think I am, an insect?" the spider stormed.

Oh no, Varun thought. Now I've upset her. Maybe she doesn't like insects. "I'm sorry, Edith. I should have counted before I spoke. Let me see. Yes, eight handsome legs."

"Don't be careless with your looking," Aubrey whispered.

Edith, who seemed to be soothed as quickly as she was angered, gave Varun another opportunity. "How do you like my web?" she asked.

Varun began to give the web his close attention. It almost filled the doorway. Threads of spider silk extended outward from the center like spokes on a wheel. Other strands of silk ran around the web in circles. The smallest circle was close to the center of the web; each circle was larger the further it was from the center. Several strands of silk anchored the web to the top and sides of the doorway.

"It's very nice," said Varun. "How did you do it?"

"It's not too hard if you have silk glands and spinnerets."

"What are they?"

The spider looked at Aubrey with two of her eight tiny eyes. "Does this boy know anything?"

"Don't be rude, Edith. Turn around."

The spider turned her back to them.

"At the back of her abdomen Edith has spinnerets. They are clusters of many tiny faucets where the silk material comes out. The spinnerets are so small you can't see them unless you look through a strong lens, but the

faucets deliver different kinds of silk that harden into threads as soon as they get into the air."

"You mean she makes the silk inside herself, like bees make wax?"

"That's right," the Elf confirmed

"But what does she use the different kinds of silk for?"

The spider turned around and stamped one leg with impatience, but Aubrey gave her a stern look. "Boys don't have silk glands, so you can't expect them to know much about spider webs. Why don't you tell him, Edith? Nicely!"

"Touch one of the silk threads running around the web in a circle, Varun. Gently!" Edith ordered.

Varun put his little finger on one of the threads. When he pulled his finger back, the thread tried to follow. "Hey, it's sticky."

"Now touch one of the threads connecting the circles — the threads that run from me out to the edge of my web."

Varun did as directed. "This one's not sticky!"

"Now do you see how I use different kinds of silk?"

"I guess the circle ones are sticky so they hold insects that fly into your web?"

"Brilliant," muttered Edith.

Conversation with Edith was proving difficult, and although Varun thought another question might annoy her, his curiosity got the better of him. "What happens when an insect flies into your web and gets caught."

Aubrey plucked one of the anchor threads on the web and caught the spider's attention with a glare.

"It makes the web vibrate," Edith purred, "so I know I caught something. Then I rush out and wrap a different kind of silk around it, so it can't struggle and break my web. And when I get hungry, I eat it."

Yuk, Varun thought to himself. But he decided not to aggravate the spider by sharing his views on eating insects. "How often do you make a new web?"

"Practically every day."

"Wow, you must use a lot of silk."

"More than you realize. When I spin a web I have to replace some of the non-sticky threads with sticky ones, but I try not to waste yesterday's web. I recycle." Recycling obviously made the spider proud.

"How do you do that?"

"I eat a lot of my own silk."

This was another moment when Varun wanted to change the subject.

The Elf read Varun's face and came to his rescue. "Spider silk looks delicate," he said, "but some threads are stronger than a steel wire of the same weight."

"You can push on one of my anchor threads," said Edith. "It will really stretch before it breaks. But don't you dare break it!"

Varun pushed on one of the threads holding the web to the doorjamb.

It did indeed stretch quite a bit, but he was careful not to push it so far as to break it.

"Thank you Edith," said Aubrey. Then, turning to Varun, "Now we have to hurry if we are going to see everything that I think will happen today."

"Thank you Edith. I hope you catch a fly for lunch. I have to go now, Goodbye." As Varun turned to leave, a crane fly flew into the web, and Edith's attention was drawn to her late breakfast.

Varun joined the Elf, who had already started back toward the terrace. "Why doesn't Edith get caught in her own web?" he asked.

"Good question. If she walks only on the threads that aren't sticky, she won't get stuck. But I think she also oils her feet."

Aubrey was now stuck in his passion for talk, and he began to describe Edith's skill as a web-mistress. "If Edith thinks a bird might see her and try to eat her, she hides at the edge of the web. She keeps a silk line fastened at the center, and it jerks if an insect gets caught. Her eyes are very small, and she doesn't see well, but she is very sensitive to anything that makes her web jiggle."

They were passing by the corner of the cottage, and Varun glanced at the Scarlet Sage. The air was still, but he was sure the Sage waved a single leaf at him. Varun stopped in his tracks and stared. Now wondering, he tentatively waved back, and the Sage nodded its head of flowers in his direction. Varun smiled.

The Elf had not stopped, and as Varun hurried to catch up, he decided to keep his little exchange with the Scarlet Sage to himself. He figured the Sage was one of the few topics Aubrey would not discuss with him.

Aubrey was going on as if nothing had happened and was now holding forth on different kinds of spiders. "Not all spiders spin webs like Edith's. Some have webs shaped like ice cream cones. The webs are slippery, and an insect has a hard time getting out before the spider catches it."

Varun was amazed how Aubrey could talk the daylight out of any subject that came up, but he was also interested, and he wondered how many different kinds of webs spiders make and if all spiders spin webs.

"Some don't," said Aubrey.

"Some don't what?"

"Some spiders don't spin webs. Trapdoor spiders live in burrows in the ground and cover the walls with silk. They use silk and dirt to make a little lid for the entrance. When ants pass by, they jump out and catch them."

They were now well on their way up the hill to the tree where the bees lived, and Aubrey was talking about wolf spiders, who hunt, and whose eight eyes are much better than Edith's, and can look in different directions at the same time. Varun's thoughts turned back to Edith. He decided that maybe her bad temper was the result of having to eat so much web silk. He was beginning to feel sorry for her when Aubrey's discourse on spiders came to an abrupt end.

They were now in the meadow near the edge of the woods. The Elf stopped and wiped his brow with his handkerchief. "It's getting warm, and look how many flowers have come into bloom since yesterday," he said.

Varun gazed at the profusion of fresh blossoms all around them. "I think the scout bees have already found them," he said. "See how many bees are here already. Does this mean we are going to have the excitement this morning?"

Aubrey maintained his aura of mystery.

"Oh, there will be some new goings-on for you to see with the honey-making this morning, but the really big excitement will only happen when everything is ready."

CHAPTER 14

The Honey Factory

It was clear that the day was going to be unusually warm. Many foraging bees were visiting the newly opened flowers and coming home with full loads of nectar and pollen.

"Are you ready to see how honey is made?" Aubrey asked.

"I sure am!"

The Elf held Varun's hand, and in an instant they were once again reduced in size and ready to enter the hive. Aubrey waved to the guards, who ignored them, and they passed quickly through the entrance.

"Time to observe again," said Aubrey. "Let's stand out of the way and watch the foragers as they come back. There will be some new things for you to see."

Each returning field bee that had visited a flower was met within a few seconds by a bee from deeper in the hive. As they put their mouths close together, Varun could not be sure what he was seeing.

"What are they doing? It looks like they're kissing."

"Guess again," said Aubrey.

"Is the field bee giving the other bee the nectar she has brought back?"

"Right. Passing it from one honey stomach to another."

"What's a honey stomach?"

"It is a compartment in front of the main stomach. It doubles as a grocery bag and a lunch box. That's where a bee carries nectar on the way back to the hive, and it's where she puts honey for fuel if she has a long flight to look for flowers."

As Varun watched, the bee taking the newly-delivered nectar went deeper into the hive and disappeared behind a comb. "I bet she is going to make honey," said Varun.

"That's right. We'll go there in a while, but first there is more to see here."

As Varun watched, more bees arrived and delivered their nectar to waiting workers. Some of them then danced to recruit more field bees, but others left the hive immediately for another load.

As he continued to watch, it seemed to Varun that each arriving field bee was waiting longer before another bee took her load of nectar. He asked Aubrey if that were so.

"Clever of you to see that. What do you think it means?"

Varun thought for a moment. "I think it means that the bees collecting nectar are bringing it in faster than the workers who make the honey can use it," he said.

"You're right," Aubrey confirmed. "Keep watching. Something interesting will happen very soon."

Not long after the Elf had made this prediction, a bee arrived from the meadow and could not find a worker to accept her nectar. She began to walk deeper into the hive, and she greeted Varun as she passed.

"Hey, isn't that Lizzy? The bee I met in your garden. It looks like she is giving up."

"It is Lizzy," agreed Aubrey. "Come, let's follow her."

Guided by the Elf's seed flashlight, they followed Lizzy to a comb where there were many open cells partly filled with honey. Some of the bees were adding drops to the cells. Varun couldn't make out what the others were doing, but many bees just seemed to be hanging out, resting.

Varun saw Lizzy was now behaving very strangely. She held her two front legs off the comb and walked stiffly on her other four legs while shaking all over. Resting bees began to stir and approach her. "Those other bees are getting interested in her," he said

Aubrey nodded. "She is doing a tremble dance. See if you can figure out why she is doing it."

"If you didn't have that light, we wouldn't be able to see what she's doing. How would the other bees know?"

"Bees make sounds that the other bees hear, and they also make odors that the other bees smell."

Varun remembered the first time they had visited the hive. The guard bees had used an odor to tell other bees to come out of the hive to defend it and had fanned the odor with their wings. "The bees must make different signals to mean different things," he said.

"Just so," agreed the Elf.

The bees that were attracted by Lizzy's tremble dance were starting to move off the comb. The bee that had shown Varun the nursery greeted Varun as she passed.

"Hi, Nicole. Where are you going?" Varun called.

"They need help at the entrance," said Nicole as she took off on a run.

"I get it. Lizzy couldn't find anyone to take her nectar, so she came back here and did that tremble dance. That's a signal to get other bees to carry nectar and help make honey."

"Good observing and good thinking," said Aubrey. "Help goes where help is needed"

Lizzy, having finally found a bee to take her nectar, waved to Varun and left for the meadow. "Awfully busy now!" she called.

By the time Varun and Aubrey had made their way back to the area around the entrance, Nicole was getting her honey stomach filled by a newly arrived forager bee.

"Cmmm, fawoe me," she buzzed, her mouth gummed up with nectar. She led the way back into the hive to the comb where newly-made honey was being stored. She moved the nectar from her honey stomach into a drop, held it in her mouthparts, and shook her head.

"She means to say she can't talk while she is doing this," said Aubrey. "We have to wait a few minutes for most of the water in that drop of nectar to evaporate."

Varun watched carefully as the drop of nectar got smaller and smaller.

"Is that all there is to making honey?" he asked.

"Oh, no! I add a couple of special ingredients while I hold the nectar in my mouth," said Nicole, now able to talk. "It's a recipe we bees have; it changes the sugar from one kind into two kinds. Soon I'll put it in one of the cells to finish."

She pointed to cells that had caps of wax on their tops. "When the cell gets full of honey, we close it. Then we have a food supply if the weather gets cold and rainy and we can't go out. Our honey is good; try some."

Varun liked honey, and had no trouble dipping his hand into an open cell and licking his fingers. "Yummy," he agreed. Remembering Lizzy's reaction when they were in the garden, he was careful not to wipe his hand on his shirt.

"And over here we have stores of pollen. It's good too. Try some."

Varun tried a bite of pollen, but he spit it out. A passing bee spoke to him sharply as she picked it up. "Let's not have any more of that untidiness in here. Someone like me has to pick up after you and carry your mess outside."

"Sorry," said Varun, and ate some more honey.

After a while the idea of a diet of honey did not seem as interesting as it had at first. In fact he was wishing he could have something that wasn't quite so sweet, so he tried the pollen again. This time it tasted pretty good.

"You're learning," said a bee who had been watching. "That's what we call a balanced diet."

The Elf was grinning from ear to ear.

Before they left the hive, Aubrey wanted to investigate a comb they had not seen previously. When they found it, he seemed pleased. There were several very large, rough, wax cells that were not built into the comb, but hung on the surface.

"What are those, Aubrey? What's in them?"

"Those are queen cells. The young larvae were fed a special diet, and each cell contains a developing queen rather than a worker."

"What do you mean by a special diet? Don't the bees live on pollen and honey?"

"When they are young larvae, they also get a small amount of stuff called royal jelly."

"What's royal jelly?"

"Workers make royal jelly, sort of like the way you make saliva. They feed it to the young larvae. When it is time to make a new queen, however, the workers put a lot of it in the cells where they want to rear queens, and that's what those larvae get to eat."

"You mean eating lots of royal jelly makes workers grow up to be bees that are able to lay eggs?" The expression on Varun's face suggested eating other bee's spit was gross.

"Royal jelly has lots of good stuff, sort of like vitamins," said the Elf with a smile.

Varun changed the subject. "I thought there was only one queen in the hive?"

"There is only one queen at a time. These cells will not open until after Hillary leaves the hive."

"Is Hillary leaving? Where is she going?"

"Ah, that is just part of the big excitement we have been anticipating, but we will have to wait until everything is ready. It will be soon, though. Come now, it's time we had some lunch. Peanut butter will taste good after all that honey and pollen you ate."

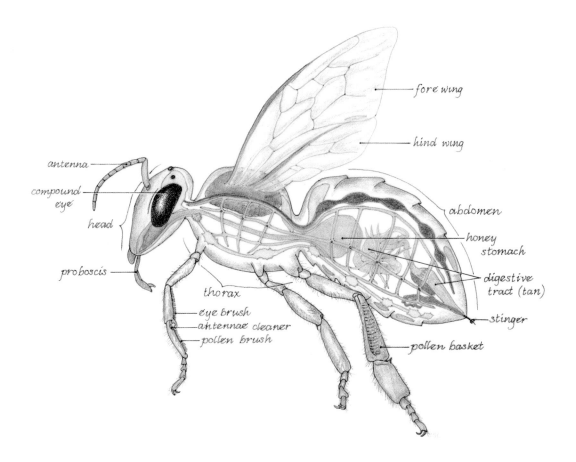

fore wing

hind wing

antenna

compound
eye

head

abdomen

honey
stomach

digestive
tract (tan)

proboscis

stinger

thorax

eye brush

antennae cleaner

pollen brush

pollen basket

When Aubrey heard that his story with Varun was going to be in a book, he thought readers like you might want to see a picture showing the parts of a bee that are mentioned in the story. For example, when Varun first met Lizzy she told him about the tools she carries on her front legs. See if you can find Lizzy's brushes and her antennae cleaner in the picture.

When Aubrey saw the picture for the first time, he pointed out that the artist had drawn interesting features that do not have labels. Here are a few things Aubrey did not have a chance to show Varun but which he wants you to know.

Insects do not have lungs. They are so small that they can get enough air through little portholes (spiracles) in the sides of the thorax. The air diffuses throughout the body through tubes (tracheae) shown here in pale blue. Bees don't have a backbone and a spinal cord like you, but they do have a nerve cord on their lower side. It's that long, lumpy yellow thing under the digestive tract. They also have blood (hemolymph), but it isn't really red as shown here in the main blood vessel of the bee. This vessel serves as a heart. It pumps the colorless or yellow blood forward and out into the tissues and recovers it in the abdomen.

CHAPTER 15

A Cool Discovery and a Narrow Escape

The Elf led the way back toward the entrance of the hive, but before they could leave, one of the bees called "Hello, Varun."

"That's Kelsey," said Aubrey. "She's up to something interesting."

Whatever she was doing was not obvious to Varun. She seemed to be just hanging around, as though waiting for a field bee to bring in some nectar or pollen.

"Hi, Kelsey. What are you doing?"

"I'm on air-conditioning duty," she said.

Now that Varun thought about it, the inside of the hive was getting very warm. But air-conditioning duty? "What does that mean? I mean what do you do?"

"We can't let it get too hot in the brood chamber, where the eggs and larvae are."

"But how do you do that?"

"With water. Right now I am waiting for a water-collector to come back from the brook with water in her honey stomach. Then I'll take it back to the brood chamber, hang it up in a drop, and fan it with my wings."

"That cools things?" Varun was skeptical.

"Well, it's not only me. A lot of my sisters are doing the same thing."

Varun pictured many bees fanning drops of water, and he remembered his first swim of the summer. He had climbed out of the lake dripping water and stood in a breeze shivering. "Oh, I see. As water evaporates, it makes you cold. That's a pretty cool way to cool the hive," he laughed.

"Here's some water now. I'm off!" Kelsey scampered to meet an arriving field bee. She took the drop of water from the other bee's mouth and immediately left for the brood chamber.

"I had no idea that bees have an air-conditioning system," said Varun.

Aubrey smiled. "Bees are a constant source of surprise. In the winter they cluster together and stay warmer than the inside of your house."

As they left the hive, Aubrey suggested they move away from the entrance so that when they returned to their normal size they would not disturb arriving bees. The Elf stopped to greet a passing ant, but Varun continued walking. He was still thinking about the bees' air-conditioning system when he became aware of a large green creature in front of him. He stopped, now frozen with fear. Two large compound eyes on a small head were watching his every movement. The creature's long spiny arms were motionless but menacing, and thoughts of a dragon leapt into his head. Ever so slowly the creature stepped toward him, and the arms moved slightly in preparation to strike. In a panic, Varun turned to run.

"Aubrey! Help!" he cried. He looked over his shoulder and saw the creature lunging for him. He felt the Elf grab him by one hand, and almost simultaneously he felt a sharp pricking in the other. The world was now rapidly shrinking around him, and then he was his normal size again, with Aubrey at his side.

"That was close," said Aubrey.

Varun felt something on his right hand and looked down to find a bright green insect, several inches long, grasping his little finger with its spiny front legs.

"This is a praying mantis," said Aubrey, as he gently detached the creature's legs from Varun's finger and held it in his own hand. He spoke to it sharply.

"Diana, what do you mean by trying to grab one of my visitors?"

"Didn't know he was with you," said Diana in a surly voice.

"What do you mean? I was right behind him."

"Didn't see you," said Diana.

"Nonsense. You have good eyes. I've a mind to glue your front legs so you can't eat for a few days."

"That would be some time out," laughed Varun. He was beginning to realize how those sharp spines would have hurt if the mantis had grabbed him when he was the size of an insect.

"Sorry," muttered the mantis. "I didn't get any breakfast this morning."

Varun shuddered. He could have been that breakfast.

"That is no excuse," said the Elf, still vexed with her.

He turned to Varun, "Predators frequently don't think before they pounce, and they certainly aren't known for good manners. I hope she didn't frighten you, but you were out of danger just in the nick of time."

"Diana, I want you to do your hunting somewhere else. I may not be around to help you if you get into trouble. And by the way, where is Roger?"

"The last I saw him he was in the bushes behind that tree." She nodded in the direction of a big maple tree at the edge of the meadow. She unfolded her wings and fluttered off, seemingly eager to get away from the Elf's scolding.

"Who is Roger?" asked Varun.

"He's another praying mantis. I think he's her boyfriend."

They climbed over the stone wall and found Roger in a small bush on the other side of the maple. He was finishing lunch, consisting of a small grasshopper that had made the mistake of hopping too close to him. Varun could see why he was called a praying mantis. He folded his front legs so it looked like he was praying. Having had both breakfast and lunch, however, Roger proved to be in a much better mood than Diana.

"I had to speak sharply to your friend Diana," said Aubrey. "She tried to snatch my companion as we ended our visit with the bees. I hope you remember not to mistreat any of my visitors when I have made them so small they tempt you."

"Me? No. I wouldn't think of it. I get plenty to eat right around here."

"Wouldn't think of it, eh? That's the trouble with you mantids. You spend a lot of time looking as though you are praying, but you are neither praying nor thinking. Be a good sport and leave my visitors alone, would you now?"

"I do my best to stay out of trouble, boss. It's grasshoppers for me."

"By the way," inquired the Elf, "How is Diana?"

"I don't see too much of her. I would rather like to give her a package of sperm, but I'm afraid she will bite my head off."

Varun thought Roger sounded sad.

"That is a problem," agreed Aubrey. "But female mantids are that way, and there is nothing I can do about it. Furthermore, I don't think counseling will help. You will have to work this out for yourself."

The mantis looked as forlorn as an insect with an armor-plated face is able to look, and it flew to another bush.

"Will she really bite his head off? I mean really truly chew his head off his body?"

"I'm afraid so. Mantids always seem to be hungry, and romance for the male is very risky."

Varun was pleased to have seen the tremble dance and how the bees make honey and air-condition the hive, but he was very glad he was not a young male praying mantis.

CHAPTER 16

Mysterious Mirrors and
a Bit of Deception

They walked along the old stone wall to the head of the path, and Varun shuddered with the memory that Diana might have eaten him for breakfast. They started down the path and had no sooner entered the field of flowers when Aubrey stopped and pointed. A hummingbird was suspended on a gentle whir of wings in front of a cluster of orange, trumpet-shaped flowers, probing with its beak.

"Hey, that's another way to get the nectar out of flowers," said Varun. "Have a long beak."

"And an even longer tongue," said Aubrey.

Varun watched the little bird as it moved among the flowers. Its wings were beating so fast they were only a blur. It reminded Varun of a tiny helicopter as it hovered in front of a flower while drinking, then scooting backwards a few inches, only to hang in the air while examining the next blossom. Every time it turned in Varun's direction, the feathers on its throat became brilliant red, but as it turned away, the color disappeared, and the throat became almost black.

"Why does it change color like that?" Varun asked. "It's really pretty when it's red."

Aubrey beckoned to the hummingbird, and it hovered in front of them. "This is a ruby-throated hummingbird," he said.

The bird was turning from side to side to show off its ruby red throat. "Ain't I handsome," he said in a thin voice, puffing out his feathers to make himself look as large as possible. "My sisters can't do this; they aren't nearly as good looking as I am."

"Why does the red on your throat change when you move around?" Varun asked.

"I do it with mirrors," said the bird, sounding smug.

"Mirrors?" Varun crinkled his forehead.

"See," said the bird, "when I turn my head, different feathers catch the sunlight. My throat feathers have a lot of tiny mirrors in them."

This still sounded strange to Varun. "But where is the red coming from?"

"My mirrors are not like the one you use when you comb your hair," said the bird. (If you ever bother to comb it, the bird thought to itself.) "They only reflect red light."

"Remember," said Aubrey, "sunlight has all the colors of the rainbow in it."

"A rainbow has all the colors spread out and separated," said Varun. "Can your feathers do that?"

"My mirrors are special," the hummingbird boasted. "Some of the colors of light that get into my feathers interfere with themselves and can't get out."

That made Varun suspicious. "What do you mean by that?"

"I mean the light going into the feathers interferes with the reflected light on its way out. It's hard to explain, but you can think about it this way," said the hummingbird. "Suppose you are trying to go into Aubrey's cottage at the same time he is trying to come out through the same door and neither of you gives way. No one gets through because you are interfering with each other. That is sort of what happens to some of the colors in my feathers. Only the red light doesn't interfere with itself like that, so it gets back out."

"The color is really bright, almost like there is a light inside," said Varun.

"That," said the bird, "is because the red light actually brightens on the way out."

"How can that be?" Varun demanded.

"Suppose you and Aubrey are going through that door in the same direction, and he is giving you a boost. You sort of pop out together. That is sort of what happens to the red light. With light it makes the light brighter."

"That's hard to understand," said Varun.

"Just remember that the red light boosts itself out, and all the other colors stumble over themselves inside," said the bird.

"Remember how sound travels in waves?" added the Elf. "So does light. Think about waves in the ocean. Waves have peaks and valleys. When waves meet other waves, sometimes their peaks can add and make a bigger wave, but if a peak on one meets a valley on the other, they can sort of cancel each other out."

This was all new to Varun. He thought he understood, but he had another question. "Is the color always red?" he asked.

"My feathers are always red, but other kinds of hummingbird have green or blue, or violet throats," said the bird. "I like mine best, though."

"Some butterfly wings and the backs of beetles have mirrors like that too," said Aubrey. "Different colors have different lengths of wave."

"I'm really busy today. Can I go now?" said the bird.

Aubrey dismissed it with a nod and a wave of his hand. "You have just met iridescence," he said.

"The hummingbird's name is Iridescence?"

"No, the hummingbird's name is Christopher. Iridescence is what that kind of reflected light is called. Now let's be on our way."

Soon they were crossing a dry part of the meadow where little grew, and a movement caught Varun's attention. He grabbed Aubrey's arm, and they both stopped. A robin-sized bird with a white breast and a necklace of two, heavy, black rings was standing about 10 feet away, watching them intently. Varun raised his arm to point, and the bird turned and began to hobble and shuffle off, dragging one wing on the ground.

"Hey, it's hurt," said Varun. "Can't we help it?"

Aubrey smiled. "She's not hurt. She's trying to deceive you, and I'd say she has managed pretty well."

"What do you mean?"

"She has a nest nearby, somewhere on the bare ground. She doesn't want you to find it. If you were a fox thinking about having her for lunch, you would be quick to follow her, and when you got close and were almost ready to pounce, she would fly away."

"You mean she isn't hurt at all? She is just pretending to have a broken wing?"

"She is fit as a fiddle."

"What kind of bird is she?"

"She is a Killdeer," said Aubrey. "Lots of birds that nest on the ground in open spaces have that trick up their sleeve, or maybe I should say up their wing feathers."

Varun winced. "I suppose next you're going to tell me she kills deer."

"Oh no. Killdeer is just what she sounds like when she calls. At least that's what some people think she sounds like, so that's how she got her name."

"Playing that trick is pretty clever," said Varun.

"Well, it's certainly effective. It's clever like a plant is clever," the Elf concluded with his accustomed air of mystery.

CHAPTER 17

The Butterfly's Tale

Varun was mulling over the riddle of animals that did clever things without being clever when they came to a stand of tall plants with dense clusters of deep pink flowers. Large, orange and black butterflies were flitting from flower to flower. "Do you remember what those butterflies are called?" Aubrey asked.

"Sometimes they come to the butterfly bush in Grandma's garden. But I forget their name."

"Monarch butterflies," said Aubrey. "And how many legs on a monarch butterfly?"

Varun hesitated. He remembered that insects have six legs, but after his foolish mistake with the spider he thought maybe the Elf was trying to trick him. He decided to count. "Hey, there's only four," he exclaimed.

One of the butterflies perched on Aubrey's shoulder and spoke in a tiny voice. "I have six legs. The front two are diminutive and I keep them tucked up so they are hard to see."

Varun turned to see who was speaking, and the butterfly continued. "My proboscis is a most serviceable instrument! Would you like to see it?"

"What is that butterfly talking about?" said Varun.

"Alexandra is a learned butterfly, and she likes to practice her vocabulary," said the Elf.

"I don't understand either one of you," said Varun.

"She likes to use big words," explained Aubrey. "Alexandra, let's show Varun what you are talking about."

The Elf squeezed a small drop of nectar out of a flower onto the tip of his finger and held out his hand. Alexandra perched on his finger, and Varun was astonished as the butterfly uncoiled its mouth into a long thin tube and sucked up the nectar.

"Hey, it's like her tongue is a drinking straw!"

"My proboscis," corrected the butterfly.

Aubrey picked a leaf from one of the plants. A white sap oozed from the base of the leaf, where it had been broken. "See this plant? It's called milkweed."

"I bet that's not really milk. It only looks like milk," said Varun.

"You're right. But milkweed is the only plant where monarch butterflies lay their eggs."

"The foregoing has been my principal undertaking during the preceding fortnight," added Alexandra.

Varun frowned, and looked at the Elf, puzzled.

"She says she has been laying eggs for the last two weeks," said Aubrey.

Alexandra stamped one of her tiny feet in impatience. "Isn't that what I told him?"

Varun ignored the butterfly, but he was curious about the plant. "Why only on milkweed?"

The butterfly's response was quicker than Aubrey's. "Because the opaque and untinted substance you observed emanating from that broken petiole is extremely distasteful, even toxic, to any avian predators so unwise as to consume me or one of my brethren."

Varun was beginning to understand the butterfly's fancy way of speaking, and confidence prompted a retort. "You mean that milky stuff doesn't taste good and makes birds sick?"

"Isn't that what I said?" grumbled the butterfly.

The Elf, who was having trouble staying in charge of the conversation, pointed to another part of the plant. "The eggs hatch into caterpillars, and here is one that has eaten a lot of leaves and grown quite big."

Varun watched the caterpillar tear off a bit of leaf with its pincer-like mouth. "Why doesn't eating milkweed make the caterpillars sick?" he asked.

"Good question," said Aubrey. "Cows get sick if they eat milkweed, and you would too if you ate some. But the caterpillars separate the poison from the rest of their food and store it where it won't be in the way."

"You mean they keep the poison in their bodies, and anything that eats them will get sick?"

Aubrey nodded.

"That's cool." Varun looked at the caterpillar with new interest. Its body was smooth, with white, black, and yellow rings running around it.

"Our conspicuous coloration is unique, and it advertises our distasteful nature," said Alexandra.

Varun, now thoroughly engaged, thought that being brightly colored did not make a lot of sense. "Being easy to see doesn't do either you or the caterpillar much good if you get eaten by a hungry bird. It seems to me you would be better off if you were hard to see."

Also warming to the subject, Alexandra forgot to put on airs. "If a bird pecks one of us, it will get sick. So sick it will remember, and it won't want to make the same mistake again. Because we are so brightly colored, both as caterpillars and butterflies, we can be easily recognized and avoided. That makes life safer for the brothers and sisters of any one of us that gets pecked. Birds can learn. Bird brains aren't as dumb as some people think."

During this exchange, the Elf had been looking among the plants, gently turning over leaves, and he now found what he was searching for.

"Look at this," he said, pointing to a small green object dangling like a Christmas tree ornament from the bottom of a leaf.

"With this new object of attention, Alexandra resumed her formal ways. "A caterpillar has withdrawn into that chrysalis it manufactured, and it is totally rearranging its morphology," she gushed.

"You mean a caterpillar is inside changing into a butterfly?" said Varun.

"That's what I just said," Alexandra snapped.

Varun gently touched the chrysalis. "Larval bees change like this too, except they stay in their cells in the honeycomb the whole time." He spotted another chrysalis that had split open, revealing a bedraggled butterfly. "Hey, here's one coming out now. It looks like it's having a hard time. Maybe we should help it." He reached to touch the emerging butterfly, but Aubrey stayed his hand.

"No, don't touch him. He needs to do it by himself, but it will take time. Watch him. He is pumping blood into his wings, and they will soon expand and dry. Then he will be ready to fly."

"Varun, don't you think we're clever?" said Alexandra. "If you didn't know how we grow and develop, you might think that caterpillars and butterflies were completely different kinds of animals." Varun agreed that a caterpillar turning into a butterfly is indeed amazing, and Alexandra turned to the Elf. "You haven't told Varun about our other mysterious and spectacular feature."

"Would you like me to tell your story?" Aubrey asked.

"That would be most agreeable," Alexandra responded.

"Do you think you can keep from interrupting?"

"I shall most certainly try, but I find the story exciting every time I hear it."

Aubrey smiled and began. "The monarch butterflies that are living at the end of summer do something that is really astonishing. They start flying south on a journey that takes them as much as 2000 miles, and sometimes over vast stretches of water, to the country of Mexico. That's where they spend the winter. So many of them gather in the same place that they make the trees look as if they were covered with orange snow."

"It is a resplendent spectacle, captivating to behold," said Alexandra, who was already finding it impossible to be quiet.

"They look so delicate. And how do they know where to go? Don't they get lost?" said Varun.

"They are indeed fragile, and the trip is dangerous," Aubrey agreed. "But many of them make it."

"My offspring will certainly accomplish the passage," said Alexandra. "They will arrive unscathed, and…"

"Shhh!" bristled the Elf. "If you want me to finish the story you simply must be quiet."

"How do they find their way?" asked Varun. "What keeps them from getting lost?"

"No one knows exactly how they navigate all that distance," said the Elf.

"I can use the sun for a compass," said Alexandra, not totally squelched by the Elf.

"Yes, you can," Aubrey agreed. "Like the bees, butterflies can tell time, and they can use the sun for a compass. In fact, they have two clocks: one in their brain and another in their antennae, and interestingly, it is the one in their antennae that resets at dawn and then allows the sun-compass to recalibrate as the sun moves across the sky during the day. But having a compass doesn't tell you which direction to go unless you know where you are in relation to your destination. There is more to navigation than just having a compass. Many animals — many birds and fish — migrate long distances each year. Many of them have little crystals of a mineral that contains iron, and these crystals enable them to detect the magnetic field of the earth. This may be part of their navigation system."

"Can Alexandra do that?" Varun asked. For once, Alexandra had nothing to say.

"There is still a lot in this world that even the Elves do not fully understand, and Alexandra won't know the whole story herself until I am able to tell her."

"It's amazing," said Varun. "And then they have to make it all the way back in the spring?" It seemed to Varun that they must if they all left in the autumn.

Alexandra was again hopping up and down with excitement, but Aubrey glared at her, and she did not speak.

"Not quite," Aubrey continued. "And that makes the story even more fascinating. In the spring, they start back, but they come only part of the way before they stop, lay eggs on milkweed, and then die."

"Oh I get it. I'll bet the caterpillars that are their children eat, grow big, turn into pupae, and become adult butterflies. Then they fly here."

"Almost right," said Aubrey. "Those butterflies, too, don't get all the way back before they stop and lay eggs. The ones that finally get here to lay eggs are the great grandchildren of the ones that flew south last fall."

"So it's their children that will be the ones to fly away the end of summer! They have never been to where they are going, but they find their way?"

The Elf nodded. "It's fascinating, and is still an unsolved mystery."

"I simply love unsolved mysteries," said Alexandra. She fluttered off to another group of flowers, calling "Farewell, Varun. *Tempus fugit.*"

As the butterfly disappeared from sight, Varun wondered again how monarch butterflies know where they are and which direction to fly to reach their far-away destination. Aubrey had said that even Elves did not understand everything there was to know. How does anyone figure out things like that? I guess that's what experiments are for, but first you have to think of the right experiments. And no one has figured out all the right experiments to do to understand how butterflies migrate.

The rest of the day passed swiftly. Aubrey introduced Varun to some ants he knew, and when they got back to the cottage, they conversed with a couple of crickets and a deer mouse that shared the cottage with the Elf. All the while Varun could scarcely keep from thinking about the next day, and what would happen when Hillary left the hive.

CHAPTER 18

Diddly and Dawdly

The next day came, as is its custom, and Varun was up almost with the sun. The Carolina wren was fairly trumpeting with its own excitement, and Varun dashed into the other room to see whether the Elf was up too. He was not only up, he had breakfast ready as well. "I think today will be the day," he said in greeting, and Varun began to eat as fast as he could.

When they left the cottage, Varun wanted to go to the shed to see if the spider still had her web in the doorway. She was putting the finishing touches on some repairs, and Varun gently tweaked one of the anchor lines. Edith wheeled about to investigate, and Varun gave her a cheery hello.

"Nice day Edith; I wish you good luck this morning."

He waved goodbye as he backed away from the web, and to his surprise Edith waved one of her eight legs at him. She's not so bad after all, he thought to himself.

He and Aubrey made their way across the meadow and up the hill to the bees' tree. When they arrived, there was a great buzzing turmoil at the entrance. Bees were leaving the hive in great numbers, flying about in the air around the tree. As Varun watched, they took off in a swarm and settled in a large mass, hanging from a tree limb about 100 yards away. Varun suddenly remembered the swarm Grandpa had wanted to show him, and he tried to see what these bees were doing. He decided that some of the bees inside the swarm must be clinging to the branch, while most of the bees were clinging to other bees that were standing on other bees, and so on.

"Is Hillary there?" he asked.

"Yes, somewhere in that crowd," the Elf responded.

"What are they going to do now? Are all those other bees going with her?"

"Yes, but they are going to stay there awhile. The scouts have some work to do, and the swarm will have some decisions to make. We'll have a better view if we join them. Let's get down to their size and find some transportation. Take my hand." In short order, Varun was again the size of a bee.

The turmoil at the entrance to the hive was now over, and most of the remaining bees had gone back to work. Some drones were standing around near the entrance, and Varun noticed that as usual they did not get involved in any of the work their sisters did.

Aubrey beckoned to two of the larger drones. "Diddly, Dawdly. I have an important job for you."

"What's that?" said Dawdly, glaring at the Elf.

"We need transport up to the swarm. How about letting us ride on your backs, and you fly up there?"

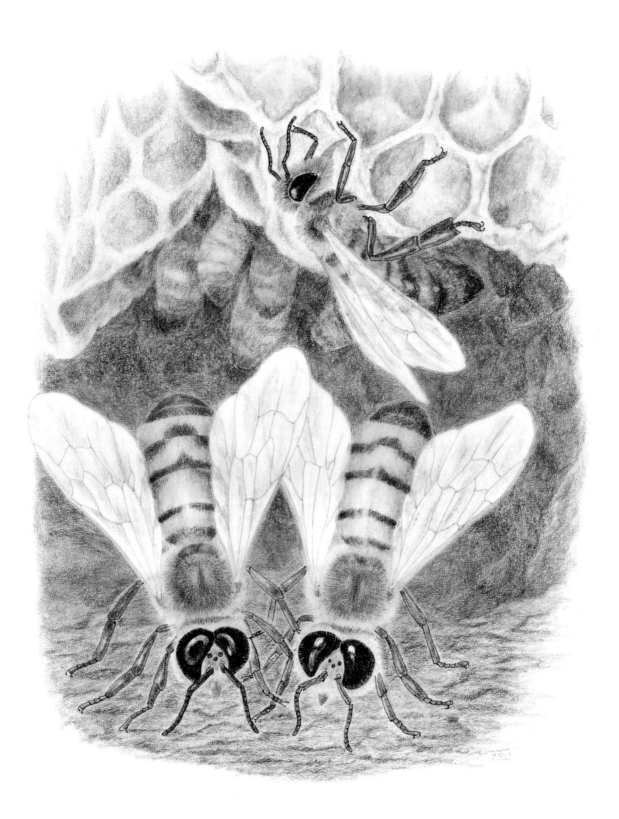

"I don't know about that," Dawdly drawled. "We want to be here when the new queen comes outside."

"That won't be until tomorrow, at the absolute earliest," said Aubrey. "You know very well she is still pupating. And anyhow, you need to find queens from other hives."

"Besides," offered Diddly, "you both look pretty heavy."

"I assure you that you will not be encumbered by the weight of a transiently diminished Elf, and Varun here will be no heavier."

"I don't much feel like it," said Dawdly. "Me neither," chimed in Diddly.

"Look, you two. I am offering you the chance of a lifetime. In the normal course of events, two weeks from now you both will be forgotten. But this morning you have the chance to be immortalized. You can be remembered for generations as the heroic pair, the Dynamic Duo of Drones, who carried an Elf and his pupil Varun on their quest for knowledge of how bees find a new home. I'll bet neither of you has any idea how your sisters do it."

Diddly and Dawdly looked at each other. Neither knew, and both were embarrassed to say so. "You say we'll be famous?" Diddly asked.

"I don't doubt it. What other drone has ever been offered such a chance? But of course if you're not up the challenge, maybe we should ask Duane and one of his friends."

"Duane!" both drones exclaimed together. "That tub of pollen? It's all he can do to get himself off the ground!" said Dawdly. "No Mr. Elf, if its Dronian Heroes you want, you've come to the right place."

"Can we start with a little practice flight?" said Diddly. "I mean, just to be sure it's going to work without crashing."

"Fine," said Aubrey. "Dawdly will take Varun and I will go with Diddly."

This pleased Diddly, who decided that he could not possibly come to harm with an Elf on board.

Varun sat astride the front of Dawdly's abdomen, just behind the wings, and hung on with his legs. The drone took off so fast that Varun thought he was going to be blown off backwards, but he managed to hang on while the drone flew out into the meadow and back.

"Dawdly, try to slow your take-offs and landings, and don't make any more sharp turns," said Aubrey, who had noticed that Varun had difficulty holding on whenever his drone felt acrobatic. "Now, let's go to that limb next to the swarm."

When the drones had delivered their riders to a tree limb next to the hanging swarm of bees, Aubrey instructed the two drones to wait, as they would be needed again. The branch was very high, but Varun found it broad enough that at his present size he could move about without danger of falling off. The day had already brought more excitement than he had anticipated.

"Observation time," said Aubrey. "Let's see what is happening."

At first Varun couldn't see much of anything happening. There was a constant buzzing, and movement of bees in the swarm, but no pattern to it. After he had watched for a while, though, he saw one, then two bees dancing on the surface of the swarm, just as he had seen bees dancing on the surface of a comb inside the hive. "Are they collecting nectar and bringing it up here?" he asked.

"No," said Aubrey. "What do you think is the most important thing for these bees to do now?"

"I guess they need to find a new place to live."

"Good guess. Right now, scout bees are looking for a new place to set up housekeeping."

"When they find a good place, do they come back and dance, just like they do when they find flowers with nectar?" Varun asked.

"Exactly so," Aubrey agreed.

"Look, there are three dancers now, and they are all indicating different directions."

As they continued to watch, a forth bee began to dance, and she was indicating the same direction as one of the first dancers. "Let's see what those two have found," said Aubrey. He called to Diddly and Dawdly.

"Drones don't know the code, so Diddly and I will lead the way, and I'll tell him what to do. Remember, Dawdly, we may have to do some searching toward the end of the flight, but there is to be no showing-off with dives and quick turns. Save that stuff to impress young queens."

CHAPTER 19

The Bees Take a Vote

Astride their drones, Varun and the Elf left the swarm, hanging high in the tree where it had settled. About half a mile from the old hive they came upon a large oak tree with a hole high up on the trunk. They could see that this was the site that the scout bees had found, for several other bees had already followed the directions given by the two dancers. Diddly and Dawdly delivered their riders to the edge of the hole and were told to wait.

Aubrey took his flashlight out of his pocket and directed the light into the cavity. Varun felt he was standing at the mouth of a large, dark cave, and he was unable to see the full extent of the hollow. He could barely make out a couple of bees down inside. "What are they doing, Aubrey?"

"When the scout bees find a possible place for the swarm to move into, they have to decide whether it is big enough."

"They don't have tape measures. How do they do that?"

"They walk around inside and explore it."

"I guess that's really important," said Varun. "All those bees in the swarm need to get in, and they are going to make comb, too. And after Hillary lays eggs there will be even more bees."

"They also have to decide whether the new place is safe. What do you think of this one?"

"I think it's pretty good because it is so high up in a tree. Most animals that will want to steal their honey will find it hard to get up here," said Varun.

"Right. It's about as large as the old hive, but it's in a much safer place," Aubrey agreed.

"The bees had found at least three places before we left the swarm. I counted three different dances pointing to different places. How do they decide which one is best?" asked Varun.

"Let's go back and see." Aubrey called for Diddly and Dawdly.

"We're getting hungry," complained Diddly.

"Take us back to the swarm, and then you can go to the hive and get lunch," said the Elf.

Grudgingly, the drones carried their two passengers back to the swarm and deposited them on the limb where they had stood previously. Aubrey now gave instructions: "One worker's honey-stomach-full of honey, and no more. I want you back here before the swarm takes off. Understand? Your Future Fame depends on it."

"You have to keep after those rascals," he said as soon as the drones had departed. "They are not very reliable."

They turned their attention to the surface of the swarm, where there were now five bees whose dances all indicated the site Varun and Aubrey had visited. Three other bees were indicating a different site. As they watched, Varun counted more dances for the favored site and some new dances for still other sites.

"But do you see anything different about the dances?" Aubrey asked. "Look carefully."

Varun continued to watch until he saw something he had not seen before. "Sometimes another bee butts one of the dancers on the head or abdomen with her own head. And sometimes the dancer stops dancing. What does that mean?"

"The scouts are among the oldest and most experienced bees in the swarm. If they have found a good place for the new home, they may try to get other scouts who have found other possible nest sites to stop dancing."

"You mean that head-butting is a signal to stop dancing?"

"Right again," the Elf agreed.

"I'll bet the scout bees follow each other's dances and examine different sites for themselves. And the dancers may change their dances if they like the new site better."

Aubrey nodded. "That's more good thinking."

"So it's sort of a vote. When most of the dancers are pointing to the same site, the bees have decided," said Varun.

"Listen. That's what's happening now," exclaimed Aubrey. "Do you hear anything above the general buzzing?"

Varun could indeed hear it. He thought he had heard it a while ago, but now it was louder: a soft sound at a higher pitch than the background buzzing. "What is it, Aubrey?"

"It's called piping. It is the signal that the scouts have agreed on the new nest site. Look at the head butting on the remaining dancers. The scouts are trying to end the searching so none of the other scouts will be left behind. Where are those drones?" he finished in exasperation.

"Right here, Mr. Elf," said Diddly, who had just landed behind him.

"And just in time. The swarm is about to move. Let's follow it and see where it's going."

"It's probably going where we took you before," Dawdly complained.

"Possibly," said the Elf. "Now be a good chap and stop fussing. We're almost finished."

The swarm began to move, and Varun had barely gotten seated astride Dawdly's back before the drone took to the air. The swarm had now detached from the limb, and all the bees were flying in the same direction. How interesting, Varun thought. The same dance is used to indicate either direction to a patch of flowers or to a new home. What it means depends on what the rest of the bees are doing at the time.

The bees were indeed going to the same hole, and after they had entered, Varun and Aubrey were deposited once more at the entrance. "They have a lot to do," Aubrey observed.

"I know. They have to start making wax comb right away, and the field bees have to start bringing in nectar to feed the others. I bet Hillary will begin laying eggs again just as soon as they have some pollen and honey and comb," said Varun.

And it all has to happen fast if the colony is to survive," said Aubrey.

"Where is Hillary now?"

"She is somewhere inside this new hive."

"What is happening in the old tree?"

"Soon now the first of the new queens will emerge from her pupal cell, and she will sting the others."

"That's mean," interrupted Varun.

"Well, that is the way it is with bees. A good observer tries to see what animals are doing without judging whether their behavior is good or bad. Good or bad is for people."

"Then she will be the only queen in that hive. I guess she will get sperm from drones and start laying eggs, and there will be two colonies and not just one," said Varun. "But I have a question. You said the animals don't talk to each other, and I only hear them talk when I am with you."

"That's right," agreed Aubrey.

"What did you mean when you said Diddly and Dawdly would be immortalized if they helped us? Bees won't be able to tell other bees about it."

"You're right; the way to be immortalized is to be remembered. Diddly and Dawdly will be remembered by everyone who hears your story when you get home or reads it if it is in a book."

Varun was pleased with that idea. The two drones would indeed be remembered if he told people what they had done. But he was still curious. "A lot of stuff the animals told me they can't really know. I mean Lizzy told me how her compound eyes work, and Christopher told me about how light interferes with itself in his throat feathers."

"Remember," said Aubrey, "perplexing things happen in the presence of an Elf." He left Varun to work that out, and looking around he called for Diddly and Dawdly. There was no response. "Drat those drones. Maybe I didn't make it clear that we need them to get us down from here. Drones have no imagination."

Varun looked over the edge of the hole. The ground was a very long way down. He was comfortable standing where he was, but he realized if he were his normal size, he wouldn't have any place to stand. For the first time all day he was scared, and his voice trembled: "How are we going to get down?"

"Hmm," said the Elf. "That is a problem."

CHAPTER 20

Friendship

Varun and the Elf were stranded high up in the new bee tree, and Varun was feeling exceedingly anxious. After a few minutes of thought, Aubrey hit upon a plan.

"Don't worry. I have a friend who lives nearby. I only hope we don't have to wait until night before she hears me." He began to call in a voice Varun could not understand. Varun was beginning to despair of all help when a small animal appeared on a limb several feet below.

"What on earth do you want, Aubrey?" it complained. "You never used to go around waking up folk in the middle of the day."

"I am sorry to disturb you Sarah, but my friend Varun and I are in a bit of a pickle. The drones that brought us up here on business have absconded, and to put it bluntly, we need your help in getting down."

"Business is it? Seems like funny business to me! But what do I know?"

The Elf waited while she stretched and yawned and muttered about being out in broad daylight. At last she pulled herself together.

"Alright, what can I do?" she offered.

"If you would climb up here so we can get on your back and hang on to your fur, you could take us down to the ground."

"Oh, that's easily done," she said, now sounding awake and actually cheerful.

Sarah scampered up the trunk. Aubrey jumped aboard and helped Varun up the animal's sleek back until he was centered and could grab a fist-full of fur in each hand. "Here we go," said Sarah, and launched into space.

Varun was terrified until he saw that Sarah was not dropping like a stone but was gliding at a steep angle away from the trunk. He peered over the side. She had a broad flap of skin between her front and hind legs, so when she stretched out her legs it made a little parachute. The realization came to him in a flash: Hey, Sarah is a flying squirrel. She doesn't really fly; she just glides from a high place to a lower one. But she sure is going fast!

He had no sooner figured this out when Sarah announced "Fasten your seat belts and prepare for landing."

"Hang on tight!" echoed Aubrey, with more practical advice.

Varun took a fresh grip of fur in each hand. Sarah came to a quick stop on the ground, and Varun was barely able to keep from pitching forward over her head. "That was really fun!" he exclaimed as soon as he had both feet on the ground.

They thanked Sarah, and Aubrey suggested she go back to bed. She assured them they had been no trouble and promptly scampered back to her hole in the tree. Aubrey took Varun's hand, and with a rush everything around

them grew smaller. Once more, in less time than it takes to tell, Varun was restored to his normal size. "That was some excitement," he said.

"It sure was," Aubrey agreed. "On the other side of the world, in places like Japan and India, there are flying squirrels the size of large house cats. The record for a long glide is more than a length-and-a-half of a football field!"

"Wow, I wish I could have that ride," said Varun.

They started down the hill together, talking about all the things Varun had seen and done during the previous days.

"What I don't understand," said Varun, "is why all of those bees co-operate with each other so well. Except for the drones, they are always ready to work together, and nobody has to tell them what to do and when to do it. I don't think people are that way."

"You are becoming a very good observer," said Aubrey. "How do you think people and bees are different?"

"People like to play and not just work, and most of the time someone is telling you what to do. But lots of time you don't want to do what other people want you to do."

"What else?"

"Bees don't talk to each other like we do. When we were just watching them, I'm sure they didn't think like we do. But their dances tell other bees important things, like where to find nectar. That's not like talking, but it's pretty complicated."

"Why do you say that?"

"It's complicated because each bee's job can change, and what their dances mean depends on what the other bees are doing. And using the sun to tell which way to go is pretty complicated too, because the directions are in a sort of code. Sometimes it is almost like a conversation?"

"How so?"

"That head-butting, when they are looking for a new place to live. It's like a group of kids trying to decide what to do next. Different kids have different ideas and try to convince each other which is best. Scouts that are trying to stop other dancers are saying, hey, look at my place."

"That is a really good analogy," said Aubrey. "But think of this. Bees and people both live in social groups. A minute ago you said people are individuals with different interests. So what holds groups of people together?"

"Well," said Varun, "they can be members of the same family."

"That's the part most like bees. Can you think of anything else?"

"People have friends, too."

"Friendship is a little bit like the relation between bees and flowers," said Aubrey.

"What does that mean? I don't get it."

"Think of it this way. Bees and flowers depend on each other. That is very important to both of them. Isn't that like having friends?"

"Well, sort of," said Varun. "But I like to be with friends because we do a lot of the same things and have fun together."

"So friendship keeps people happy? Is that all it does?"

Varun thought for a moment. "No. Friends help each other, too." He brightened. "Sarah is your friend, and she rescued us from the bee tree. I bet you'll do her a favor whenever she asks."

"And returning the favor would make me happy," said the Elf. "But aren't people sometimes mean to each other? Can't even friends be mean?"

"Yes, but people who are mean all the time don't have many friends," said Varun.

"That's right," said the Elf. "But here is the reason for friendship. Co-operating and helping each other is just as important as having fun together. It's what holds groups of people together. Friendship makes the world work."

"I'd never thought about it that way," said Varun. "Having friends is pretty important."

They walked in silence for a time, each with his thoughts.

"I have so many questions," said Varun. "When we were in the bee tree the first time, you said many plants and animals seem to be clever because so many things they do are useful, but they can't think and plan. I don't understand how that works"

"That is a long story," said the Elf. "But it goes to your question of what keeps the bees together. Do you know what evolution is?"

"I think it means the world is very, very old, and animals and plants change," said Varun.

Aubrey nodded. "Most of the kinds of plants and animals that ever lived have become extinct."

"A long time ago there were dinosaurs, and then they all died. I think people weren't around then." said Varun.

"Right," agreed Aubrey, "but evolution continues to make new kinds of plants and animals, but it happens very slowly. In fact, birds are descendants of dinosaurs. What do you think is the most interesting thing about evolution?"

"I'm not sure. Making new plants and animals?"

"It makes very complicated things."

"Bees are pretty complicated. You mean evolution is how they got that way? So complicated they seem to be clever?"

"Just so," said Aubrey.

"That means evolution has made butterflies that migrate, and bees that aren't mean to each other – except to their brothers – and spiders that spin webs, and even people who need friends to be happy," said Varun.

"All that, and much, much more," said the Elf.

Varun sighed. "I guess there's a lot to understanding how the world works."

"But you're making a terrific start."

The Elf stopped and cocked an ear as though listening, but Varun could hear nothing.

CHAPTER 21

Coming Home

The rich, musical song of a bird drifted on the still afternoon air, now closer, and Varun could just barely hear it. The Elf leaned forward, working to catch every note.

Varun was fascinated every time he saw how the Elf's pointed ears swiveled and jerked, but now he cringed, remembering their first meeting, and his empty-headed question about why Aubrey's ears were so big. His unease faded, though, as the bird came closer, and its song aroused a happier memory.

"That's the voice like a flute," said Varun. "It's the wood thrush."

"Shh," said Aubrey. He listened to another fluting phrase and smiled. "Come, he says it's time to get ready."

"Get ready for what?"

"You'll see soon."

They resumed their way, and Varun's store of unanswered questions about the previous days overcame his curiosity about the thrush's message.

"There's something else I don't understand. Both you and the Scarlet Sage said I was on a quest. What did that mean?"

"What do you think a quest is?"

"Those knights of King Arthur's Round Table were always going on quests. They were looking for something called the Holy Grail. I think that was some sort of cup. I don't think they ever found it, but they had a lot of adventures."

"You've been having adventures. Have you been searching for something?"

"I think I have been finding out things: lots of cool stuff about all sorts of things."

"Have you discovered anything about yourself?"

Varun thought long and hard before answering. "After I met William, you said there were many kinds of cool things. I think figuring out how things work is cool, not just video games, but things you see every day, if you look. You said you can't really see unless you look, but I found out that's just the start, because you also have to think. And if you can't figure things out, you can ask questions, and I guess that means if you can't find somebody who knows, you can try to find the answer in a book or maybe on the web, because knowing how things work is fun. And I found out that there are some things that nobody knows how they work, but there is a way to figure them out. That's called an experiment, and I actually did one, and it wasn't too hard."

"So a quest is really about asking a lot of questions?" Aubrey asked.

"Hey, I never thought about it that way!"

"I'd say you've had a pretty successful quest, but your real quest is now before you. Remember, figuring out how the world works is a quest, a quest for understanding. Understanding brings you wisdom. Wisdom and understanding make you a very special friend for others to have."

The new hive was far enough from the old one that they were traveling a path Varun had not been on before. They had now reached the road leading back to the cottage. Aubrey held out his hand for a high five, and Varun responded in kind. "The thrush says the time has come for me to leave you, my friend."

Varun was alarmed by at being left alone. "But how will I get home?"

"Don't worry. Look there." The Elf pointed up the road toward the cottage. Varun could see a person in the road, walking toward them. He was wearing a broad-brimmed hat like the one Grandpa wore on sunny days, and Varun thought it looked like Grandpa. He turned to ask Aubrey, but the Elf had vanished. Varun looked back to the road and saw it was Grandpa. He ran to meet him.

Suddenly there was a bright light in his eyes. The sun was shining through the bedroom window. A Carolina wren was announcing the morning from the horse chestnut tree by the window, a song sparrow was singing in the shrubs below, and he could hear the flute-like call of a wood thrush in the woods behind the house. His mother was shaking him. "Varun, it's morning. I don't think you've ever slept so late in your life."

"I've had the strangest, most wonderful dream. There was an Elf named Aubrey. And my cousins Lizzy and Nicole and Kelsey were there. But they weren't really. They were bees. Some of the bees danced, and there was a praying mantis that almost grabbed me. And a plant that wrote me a letter, but I think Aubrey really wrote it. And there were lots of other things too."

"Come and have some breakfast, and you can tell us all about it."

Grandpa and Grandma were waiting for him at the breakfast table. "I hear you've had an adventure. We would enjoy hearing about it," Grandma said.

Varun could hardly eat for telling them all about the Elf, the Scarlet Sage, the bat, the butterfly, the spider, the hummingbird, the flying squirrel, the praying mantis, the killdeer, and particularly the bees, and everything he had seen and discovered. Everyone except Grandpa expressed astonishment at how much he knew about all these creatures. At last he paused and picked up the toast on his plate. With a start he recognized the plate that Grandpa had shown him – was it only yesterday? He knew that cottage; it was the Elf's! His eye fell on the two tiny figures on the road: the one with the big hat close to the cottage, and the smaller one further down the road. He looked up at Grandpa. Grandpa smiled, and winked, and Varun was sure Grandpa's ears were twitching, ever so slightly.

Fin

About the Author

Tim Goldsmith taught biology at Yale University for over 40 years. During his last decade of teaching he brought biology to students whose primary interests lay in the humanities and social sciences. He has also been involved with reform of science education: chairing a national study of science teaching and learning in K-12 in the complex environment of public schools, and serving on the Board of The Biological Sciences Curriculum Study, a non-profit that develops innovative curricula and improved teaching methods. He and his wife Mary Helen live in Northford, CT and summer on Quissett harbor in Falmouth on Cape Cod.

About the Illustrator

Julia S. Child is a biological illustrator and natural history artist. She works in pen and ink, colored pencil, half-tone techniques, and watercolor wash, and her work has appeared in more than a dozen books and numerous scientific journals and textbooks. She lives with her husband Frank in Woods Hole, Massachusetts, where she teaches popular classes in drawing plants and animals to students of all ages.